Lies, Loss, and Longing

Lies, Loss, and Longing
English language edition copyright © 2013 The Lontar Foundation
Copyright to the English language text for the various short stories
held by their respective translators
Publication history for the short stories and their translations
may be found in the back of the book

Publication of the Modern Library of Indonesia Series, of which this book is one title,
has been made possible by the generous assistance of The Djarum Foundation.

Template design by DesignLab; layout and cover by Cyprianus Jaya Napiun
Cover illustration: detail from Long Walk to Freedom by Sutjipto Adi
image courtesy of the OHD Museum of Modern & Contemporary Indonesian Art

Printed in Indonesia by PT Suburmitra Grafistama

ISBN No. 978-602-9144-31-4

MODERN LIBRARY OF INDONESIA

PUTU OKA SUKANTA

Lies, Loss, and Longing

Translations by
Vern Cork, Leslie Dwyer, Keith Foulcher,
John H. McGlynn, and Mary Zurbuchen

Introduction by
Degung Santikarma and Leslie Dwyer

LONTAR

Jakarta, Indonesia

Contents

Introduction

Wound and Witness: Writing in the Aftermath of Violence

Putu Oka Sukanta came of age as an artist during one of the headiest, and most horrific, eras of Indonesian history. Born into a high-caste Balinese family in 1939, Sukanta began writing poetry and short stories while still in high school. The Bali of his youth was a time of idealistic struggle, with Balinese intellectuals questioning taken-for-granted hierarchies of caste and class and debating their place in the new nation of Indonesia. Sukanta left Bali to continue his studies in the university city of Yogyakarta, later moving to the urban capital of Jakarta where he taught high school and fell in with a group of progressive artists and writers. Sukanta never formally joined the Indonesian Communist Party, at that time the third largest communist party in the world, but he sympathized with its aims of moving Indonesia past its feudal history and many of his friends and colleagues were members of LEKRA, the People's Cultural Institute, a communist-affiliated cultural group that was working to imagine a modern socialist nation. In 1965, at the height of the Cold War, when right-wing military forces led by soon-to-be-president Soeharto wrested control of the country, using the pretext of an alleged communist coup to slaughter some one million accused leftists, Sukanta found himself targeted. Although he escaped with his life, he was detained without trial in Jakarta's infamous Salemba Prison. During his ten years of in jail, Sukanta continued to create poetry and fiction, often writing words inside his head when guards denied him pen and paper. Amidst the madness of torture and brutal deprivation, writing, Sukanta says, served as his"therapy."

For Sukanta, as for hundreds of thousands of other Indonesians marked with the state stigma of "ET" or "ex-political prisoner," release from prison did not mean freedom. Under Soeharto's New Order regime, which lasted from 1966 to 1998, former prisoners were kept under strict surveillance, required to report regularly to the military. Sukanta was luckier than some: using the acupuncture skills he had learned from a Chinese fellow prisoner, he was able to support himself as a healer, although he ran afoul of the authorities for providing treatment to other former detainees, many of whom struggled to survive in the face of intense discrimination. After publishing his first collection of poems in 1982, Sukanta was invited several times to read his work overseas, but on returning home he would inevitably be arrested and interrogated. It was only with the fall of Soeharto's New Order regime, and the gradual opening of public spaces for acknowledging histories of violence, that Sukanta was able to write and practice without fear.

Intensely prolific, Sukanta has spent the post-Soeharto years publishing numerous collections of poetry and short stories, garnering increased international recognition, most notablya the Hellman-Hammett Human Rights Watch award for writers who have been targeted for persecution. He has been deeply involved in efforts to address the human rights abuses of the Soeharto regime, directing an oral history project to collect testimonies of survivors of the 1965-66 violence, whose narratives were suppressed by the state. Sukanta has also continued his work as a healer, founding an organization devoted to promoting Indonesian traditional medicine. The art of healing provided Sukanta with another way to enact the social justice commitments so evident in his writing. Treating the most marginalized members of Indonesian society, especially the HIV-positive, and teaching the poor to use Indonesia's store of medicinal plants and traditional remedies, Sukanta has continued to give voice to the hurts and hopes of the excluded.

The short stories gathered in this collection reflect Sukanta's diverse experiences and deep dedication. Many of them portray the experiences of survivors of violence: their losses, their desires, and the memories that fragment an official forgetting. Yet one of the great strengths of Sukanta's writing is that it avoids, for the most part, the kind of bombastic sloganeering or uncritical sentimentality that characterizes a fair amount of commentary, artistic and otherwise, on 1965-66. Sukanta's aesthetics and politics are intimate ones, concerned with taking the reader inside the everyday lives and labors of his characters, including their struggles to put pain into words. In "Storm Clouds over the Island of Paradise," Sukanta tells the tale of a young, high-caste Balinese woman who falls in love with a commoner man. It's a romantic tale in which true love triumphs, but at the same time it unflinchingly exposes the inequalities of caste and gender that lie behind the touristic myths of a Balinese paradise. In "Pan Blayag," the story of a horse-cart driver who hopes an asphalt road will change his life, Sukanta brilliantly conveys the wild promises and bitter disappointments of New Order development strategies that privileged the elite and left ordinary people behind. In "Luh Galuh," a Balinese woman is widowed by the 1965 violence, then left impoverished when the gleaming machines of the so-called Green Revolution replace her work in the rice fields. Neglected by her family—except when they need her to make offerings to the gods for Balinese rituals—the elderly Luh Galuh is finally captured by the blind eye of a tourist's camera that frames her as an icon of timeless traditional simplicity, misrecognizing her very modern suffering. And in "Bridge of Light," Sukanta writes from the perspective of a former political prisoner who visits the Soeharto-era monument to its "triumph" over communism, Jakarta's still-extant Museum of Communist Treachery. There he meets a woman who, it turns out, is the daughter of a military general revered as a national hero for his alleged martyrdom at the hands of depraved communists. Neither character believes the histories on display, but neither can they communicate openly. Yet across the political gulf that separates them, they see each other illuminated in their humanity, linked in a flashing moment that exposes all Indonesians as victims of violent deceit.

As a Balinese writer, Sukanta is challenging in his perspective. While many Balinese have produced highly critical works, most of these have taken the form of nostalgic lament for a traditional Bali in danger of touristic overdevelopment. Sukanta's eye is far more penetrating, recognizing the inequalities that are lauded in the name of "Balinese culture," strengthening a hierarchical caste system and justifying the oppression of women, the poor and those who would speak out. Despite the fact that some 80,000 to120,000 were killed during 1965-66 in Bali alone, Sukanta is one of only a handful of Balinese literary figures to address this bloody history. He does this not merely by exposing the existence of the mass graves that rest underneath the island's fabled beaches and hotels, but by drawing links between the violence of the past and the ongoing pressure for Balinese to perform an image of peace and harmony, often at the expense of their own honesty and dignity. As an Indonesian writer, Sukanta is likewise eloquent on the subject of injustice, introducing us to characters whose everyday lives fail to mirror the grand vision of Indonesian nationalism. Writing in the tradition of Indonesia's foremost literary figure, Pramoedya Ananta

Toer, Sukanta delves deeply into ordinary suffering, using his keen eye for the mundane to expose extraordinary contradictions. Many of Sukanta's stories end in sadness: Pan Blayag is left cursing at the wind and Luh Galuh is waiting for a recognition that seems unlikely to come. At the same time, there is a strength in Sukanta's characters that gives them, and us, insight into their predicaments and the changes that must happen in Indonesia. Sukanta refuses to mythologize Indonesia's past, but neither does he lead us into despair over its future. But it is as a writer whose work transcends location that Sukanta is perhaps best appreciated. The wounded longing he evokes in these stories—longings for justice so often denied, longings for connection across differences, longings for a clear vision forward—are those we all can share.

Leslie Dwyer and Degung Santikarma

The Paper Round

He's up again this morning before the sun. Sometimes he's even out of bed before the birds have left their nests in search of food. He heads off on his squeaky bike towards the southern part of town, breathing in the freshness of the cool morning breeze. It makes him feel better about having to go and get the job done.

The creaking noises coming out of his old bike mirror the complaints of his body, never really rested, never properly looked after. But he never says no when there's this out-of-hours work to be done.

He makes it to the first house, leans his bike gently against the wall, and slips a newspaper under the door. There's no answer from inside, so he heads off on the trail of the other houses on the daily round. At house number three, he wonders for a moment whether he should leave a paper or not. "This comrade always has trouble coming up with his payments," he reminds himself.

He agonizes over what to do, but then suddenly thinks of the man's job: he's just an office messenger, probably not earning enough even to feed his family. "But he needs to read *The People's Daily*," he decides. So, in the end, he passes a copy of the paper through the opening in the door.

By the time he reaches the tenth house, the sun is just starting to redden the edges of the roof.

"You're early today," says the comrade in the twelfth house on his route. "Aren't you supposed to be teaching?"

He hands the man a paper. "I had to fill in for my brother. He went to some official function last night and he still isn't home."

His comrade takes the paper and, after looking at the date on it, says, "Where's the one from the day before?"

"This is all there was when I picked them up from the post office last night," he says. That seems to satisfy the man, and he moves on the next house on his route, hoping to get most of the papers delivered before 7:00 AM. By the time he reaches the crossroads, it's already ten to seven. He looks at the bundle of papers still tied to the carrier on the back of his bike, and his weary eyes estimate the number of papers yet to be distributed. But at this hour of the morning he has no choice but to leave this job and move on to the next. He peddles the creaky old bike to the school where he teaches.

One of the other teachers calls out, "So you're still doing that paper round?"

"Well, yes, my brother's busy with something else," he replies casually.

"Some people have no shame, do they? Here you are, a teacher, and you're off working as a delivery boy as well. Why don't you look for something better?" jokes his friend. But it's not the first time he's had this kind of ribbing, from other teachers as well.

"What do you make as a delivery boy?" asks his friend. He controls his urge to say something, but the man keeps it up. "Great. Things are so bad that teachers have to do paper rounds. I wouldn't mind doing one myself, especially if I could work for *The People's Daily*."

The sarcasm makes it impossible for him to restrain himself. "Look, I'm not in it for the money."

"In that case, what are you doing, taking on a paper round that sometimes makes you late for school?"

He's sorely tempted to tell the man what an idiot he is, but he holds his peace. He doesn't have the heart to let fly at him. "It's all right," he thinks. "He just doesn't understand. It will mean more if I explain it to him." So he calmly tells his fellow teacher what the paper means to him, and what it means for the revolution. But before his friend has the chance to take it all in, they hear the bell ring. "We'll talk more about the bigger things later. I want to tell you what it's like to try to be a good revolutionary," he says. There's no reply.

The afternoon sun is starting to burn his skin, but he's still not ready to head for home. One by one he ticks off the houses of each of the subscribers on his round, till finally at three in the afternoon he turns his bike in the direction of home. The stack of papers he's been carrying since early morning is gone, and he's already making plans to deal with the next lot that should have just arrived.

Later that afternoon he calls at the post office, only to find there's nothing for him. Over the next few days it's the same story, and his older brother, the regular delivery man, is still busy with party work. To him, it's all the same: all of it work in the interests of the party. He never thinks about whether one sort of work is harder than another, but he does worry about his little brother, taking over his paper round whenever he's away and teaching as well.

"What if we give the job to someone else?" he suggests.

"Why would we do that?"

"Well, you've seen how it goes. I've often got other jobs to do, and you know that my family couldn't survive on what I get from the paper round. I'm going to look for another job, even though I'll keep doing these other things as well."

"But we can keep up the paper round, even if we both have other jobs. It's not just a matter of money. It's more about how we can serve the party by getting out these papers everyone needs to read."

"But you know what it's like, taking over my round when you still have to teach. I think it's too much for you."

"It's not too bad. We have to do something else to make money. Neither of us can feed a family on what a delivery man makes. But when it comes to party work, I couldn't bring myself to stop the paper round. That's something I want to keep up."

In the end they agree to keep up the paper round as a way of helping the party out. The crucial role that *The People's Daily* plays seems increasingly evident to them, and out of love for the party they put aside any talk of not going on with the deliveries.

It's now several days that he's been going to the post office for nothing. So, late one afternoon, he calls in at the local party committee office, to see what's been causing the hold up.

Responding to his query, one of the committee members who works for *The People's Daily* tells him: "Listen, if that's the case, I think I had best go to the airport and ask what the problem is. It'd be good if you came too," the man suggests. "That way, you can tell the subscribers what's going on."

The next day, with letters of authorization from the agent, they head off to the airport. There they show their letters to someone in the warehousing department, but it's still not simple.

"I don't have the authority to hand anything over to you," the official informs them. "You need to get permission from my section head. But he's on leave at the moment, at home."

"But you can see that this delivery is for me. I just want to pick it up here instead of having to go through the post office."

"I don't have the authority."

"How long have those papers been here?"

"A week or so, I guess."

"So why haven't they been passed on to the post office?"

"That's not my concern. My job is just to open and close this place."

The wrangling goes on until almost closing time. Finally, they manage to extract the back issues of the newspaper from the warehouse and load them onto their bikes.

They grumble to each other all the way back.

"The reactionaries are doing all they can to sabotage our work. Look at any bus stop: all the other papers from Jakarta are no more than two or three days old. But when it comes to *The People's Daily* it can be up to ten days, or sometimes they just don't come at all. They just wait until it's time to bury them all."

The heat of the afternoon sun gradually silences their complaints.

That same day, in the late afternoon, he and his brother divide the bundles of newspapers between them. He sets off on his rusty old bike to deliver the papers to subscribers in the northern part of town, while his brother heads for the homes of subscribers in the south.

When he starts handing over five issues of the paper at once, the incredulous look he's given is always the same.

"What's the matter?" he asks one of the subscribers.

"What do you mean? Sometimes the paper doesn't come at all and now we get five issues all at once. How am I going to get through them all? What's going on? There's never any problem with the other Jakarta papers."

He's reluctant to respond to the complaint, but in the end he gives in and explains what the problem is. At another house on the round there's another complaint: "I never know when the paper's going to turn up, but the bill always comes on time. I think this time I'll pay this month's subscription next month."

Keeping his feelings to himself, he goes on to the home of the next subscriber.

When one of the subscribers tells him what the delays mean to him, his old enthusiasm for the job is fired up again: "If a day goes by without *The People's Daily*, I feel like I'm going blind. I'm really hooked on it. Sometimes it makes me distrust everything I read in the other papers. But why is there so little reporting of what's happening here? Don't we have any reporters here?"

"We've got some, but they get tied up with other things that take up all their time. I think it would be good if every one of our comrades here helped them out by sending in local news reports. That way, I'm sure the important things happening here would make it into the paper more often."

"I'll see what I can do about the delays, find out what can be done to speed them up and make them more efficient. I was over in Banyuwangi recently, and the papers there were only three days old. The best we seem to be able to do here is ten days."

"I don't know what to do about it either."

With readers and subscribers like that, he keeps up his energy for the job. If only they were all as accommodating, it wouldn't feel like such hard work riding his bike all over town to deliver papers in good time.

With the pile of papers on the carrier now all gone, the squeaky old bike slowly heads for home. But suddenly, three kilometers or so from his destination, the bloated tires on the bike decide to pop. It comes as a shock, and hardly believing it's possible, he squats down and rubs his hands over them. They're completely flat.

With empty hands in his pockets, and taking one slow step after another, he finally sees his house drawing near.

Pan Blayag

The people of Dangin Bukit village scattered like bees from a hive. The village meeting at the *balai banjar*, the community meeting hall, was over but there was still the sound of grumbling in the air as people groused about the decisions that had been made.

Pan Blayag, paying no attention to the others, hurried for home. His water buffalo was sure to be hot and thirsty. The meeting had been too long. The votes had fallen short of consensus. But a feeling of satisfaction kept him from griping. Even though he hadn't contributed his opinion, he could accept the explanation of the village head and agree with the decision that had been made. The muddy dirt road that cut through the neighborhood was to be repaired immediately; the government would put in a smooth asphalt road. The makeshift wooden bridge the villagers had built was to be replaced by one of concrete.

These improvements were taking place not because the people of the village had asked for them, but because a waterfall at the foot of the hill, at the mouth of a ravine, was to be turned into a tourist attraction. The waterfall, as long as a demon's tongue, was to be converted into cash. This meant that the road had to be widened and smoothed, which meant that the villagers who lived along the road would have to sacrifice a strip of one or two meters of their land.

Arriving home, Pan Blayag found his son playing marbles by the side of the road. "Where's the water buffalo?" he asked. "Did you already move him out of the sun?"

"Yes, I did."

Pan Blayag didn't go directly to the field behind his house where he tethered his water buffalo. Instead he headed for the bullock cart, still splashed with mud from his trip to the market earlier that day. He had returned to the house by nine o'clock so as not to be late for the meeting at the *balai banjar*, which was scheduled to start at eleven. The meeting was an important one, he had been told, and heads of households who didn't attend were to be fined. While that practice was customary, this time the fine would be twice as much as usual.

The trip to the market was a daily event and Pan Blayag had to be up by three in the morning in order to make the rounds of his village with his buffalo and cart to gather the charcoal or the harvest produce that was to be sold at the morning market, which took place from before dawn until six in the morning.

The morning market was held at the intersection of the village road with the main road, where traders from the city waited with vans and pickup trucks to buy local produce. The traders weren't about to use their vehicles to go straight to the village, not with the condition of the village road: rutted, muddy, and narrow. The bullock cart was the only way to convey the produce for sale. Even so, as a bullock-cart driver, Pan Blayag could barely make a living from his trade.

Pan Blayag stood beside the cart, parked under a jackfruit tree by the side of the road. Its worn iron wheels betrayed its age. Its grimy spokes reminded him of how he always had to travel down that muddy road.

"In a little while you won't have to get all dirty," he said, patting the wheel. "The trip will be faster, and the buffalo's burden will be easier." He spoke to himself, as he swept the charcoal dust from the back of the cart.

That evening, he told his wife about the meeting. There was fire in his eyes as he spoke.

His wife replied in astonishment: "They're going to take two meters of our land for the road? Why doesn't the government give us compensation?"

"Everybody has to contribute for the road. What's two meters compared to the increase in the value of our land?"

"How will the value increase?" Her disbelief was apparent in the tone of her voice.

"If the value of our land now is, let's say, 500 rupiah a meter, once there's an asphalt road, the value will go up to 2,000 rupiah a meter at least. We'll make a profit, you know, if we ever want to sell it.

"I don't agree. Why would we sell our land? The money would just get spent."

"Who said we want to sell our land? What I mean is that we won't lose by donating two meters of land for the road. Imagine how much more busy the village will be. There will be non-stop traffic in front of our house. You can open a shop for the tourists who come to see the waterfall. Maybe our village will even buy a set of gamelan instruments and train dancers. There's a lot of beautiful girls around here."

"What kind of shop could I have? And where would I get the money to start it?"

"Later on we'll see about what to sell. And the money? We'll put aside a bit of what I get. Once the road's been paved I'll be taking even more loads, because I'll be able to make several trips every day."

The days sped by until five years had passed, and what Pan Blayag predicted would happen had failed to come true.

Since the night before, the rain hadn't stopped, only tapered off briefly. Even though it was almost noon, the sun couldn't escape from the mass of clouds in which it was blanketed. Pan Blayag was hanging around on the leaky porch of his house, wrapped in a patched, threadbare sarong. For the past year, his oxcart had sat by the side of the house, where the termites had feasted on it. One of its wheels had broken and come loose. His wife had never opened the shop they had once spoken of. But the smooth asphalt road wound its way like a snake through the village, and the traffic of motorcars never stopped crawling along it.

"There's no rice," came the voice of Pan Blayag's wife from inside the house. "All we have is cassava."

"Just charge it at Pak Amin's food stall."

His wife's reply went unheard, drowned, perhaps, by the sound of a passing truck, which splashed water from a pot-hole onto the terrace of the house as it raced by. It was the same house as before, only now it sagged to one side.

"Where is that land broker?" Pan Blayag muttered. "What's happened to him?"

"How did your discussion go yesterday?" called his wife from inside.

"He offered 100,000 rupiah per hundred-square meters."

"All right, then; take it. I want to move. We could die here with things like this. What's there to live from?"

"I'd hoped that the asphalt road would turn our village into a town, that there would be electricity and running water, that we'd all become city people," said Pan Blayag.

"Well, that's happened already," said his wife.

"But those damned trucks and mini-vans have killed our business. Damn! There's no one left here who wants to use an oxcart to transport their goods—and that's all we have to offer."

"What happened to those plans to open a shop?"

"The devil with that! Don't even think about it. It pains my heart to see all those city people coming here to buy land and opening up businesses with more money than I can count. Look at all the buildings around here: the stores and the repair shops…. Who owns them? Newcomers, all of them. And of the original villagers there's only a few of us left."

"Stop complaining. It's just lucky that we didn't rush to sell our land like so many others. Look at them now. Their land is gone, and their new businesses went bankrupt after just a couple of months. Their new motorcycles are broken down and they don't have the money to fix them. The few remaining villagers are lining up for the transmigration program. Our village has been invaded by city people."

"Yes, we'll have to move to the country if we want to stay alive."

"But move where?"

"To the top of the hill over there. We'll buy land there. We're farming people. Living in town doesn't suit us."

"But what about I Blayag? What about his school?"

"To hell with school. Even if he can't read and write, he has a better chance of becoming someone if his arms are strong enough to swing a hoe. Besides, he's not going to get a job in an office just by graduating from primary school."

The rain began to calm, but the sky stayed dark. Pan Blayag writhed and fumed. He stepped to the edge of the porch and his gaze fell on the oxcart.

"You belong on a rutted, muddy road. Not a smooth asphalt road."

He turned a furious glance toward the road that faced him. And as a truck glided past, loaded with cargo, he cursed it, crying "Robber!"

But nobody heard his voice. It echoed in the lonely chambers of his heart.

Storm Clouds over the Island of Paradise

Waiting on the shore at the port of Ketapang, Tini gazed far into the distance, trying to penetrate the black curtain of night obscuring her view. The shimmering lights on the opposite shore indicated that life was going on over there, but she wasn't sure exactly where the ship was going to take her. The lamps to her left twinkled like a group of fireflies against the dark of the earth. So, too, did the lamps on her right, reaching into the distance in silence. Which side were the beaches of Bali on, she wondered.

Even if the deep blue sky had been clear and filled with stars, she wouldn't have known at which end Gilimanuk was. She saw nothing except the vague outline of a row of hills resembling a fort. And there at the foot of the hills the lights twinkled. Whether they were the lamps of fishing boats or of houses near the beach, she didn't know. The opaque blue sea lay spread out like a carpet.

Reluctant to leave the shores of Java, she hesitated before heading for the ferry waiting to take her across the straits. The bus that had brought her from Jakarta was queued up with others to go on board. And on the bus was her mother.

She felt isolated among the crowd of passengers as she climbed reluctantly to the upper deck of the ship. Most of the other passengers, too drowsy to stir, had remained in the buses; but there were still a few who went up to the waiting lounge on the upper deck, eager to enjoy the sea breeze.

Tini felt so alone. Alone in her loneliness. Estranged. She found a seat at the end of an empty bench and sank into the silence of the night and the dim, quiet shadows of the hills.

When at last the ship moved off, she watched as the beach of Ketapang drew further and further away. She wrapped her arms around herself, feeling her hair tousled by the wind, her eyes swimming with tears. She tried hard to contain her emotions, but inside she whispered: "Good-bye, freedom." She glanced at her watch. It was five minutes past midnight.

When she looked at the time again, it was twelve-thirty. The ship had berthed at the port of Gilimanuk, and the passengers stared out at a Balinese split gate.

"Are these the gates to a *pura dalem*?" Tini thought to herself— the temple that was the resting place for the souls of those who have just died?

"It could be, too," she thought. "I'm lying here on this earth with no strength, even though fresh blood pulses through my veins. I'm a living corpse. My heart is being murdered." And the moment her feet touched the ground of the Island of Paradise, her heart screamed out in rebellion: "Why did I have to be born as the high-caste Brahman Ida Ayu Ketut Sumartini? Why not just plain ordinary Ketut Sumartini? Why do I have to bear the noble title Ida Ayu? Why?"

She stepped up into her bus and sat next to her mother, sinking back in the seat. She closed her eyes, but found it impossible to sleep. Warm tears seeped through her lashes. With her eyes tightly shut, she felt as if there was a firm arm around her shoulders. She heard a voice filled with love whispering to her.

"Whatever your mother does to us is only an obstacle for us to overcome. It all depends on the two of us. What power on earth can separate our hearts?"

Tini swallowed her tears. Loving fingers brushed her cheeks, her hand was held in the warmth of his. She rested her head on his shoulder. Feelings of anger and love rose in her heart. She felt his gentle kisses on the crown of her head.

"Until now we've been winning this struggle. The sorcerer they consulted hasn't succeeded in separating us. They'll never succeed as long as we remain firmly united. And we've overcome the last magic token. No tricks of black magic will ever defeat the purity of our feelings."

The voice, full of confidence, echoed in her ears. She opened her eyes to see the man she loved, but he wasn't there. All that remained was a beautiful memory giving her the strength to continue to love.

She smiled a little, thinking of all that had happened. Ever since her family learned that she was in a relationship with a man of a lower caste, almost all her relatives had shown hostility toward her—especially her mother, and the aunt in whose house she was living. She received letter after letter from Bali, all of them filled with the same advice: don't do what you know is wrong. In other words, have nothing more to do with that low-caste man: find someone else of your own caste. Then when she had shown no signs she was going to change, strange things began to happen.

On returning home from classes at the university, she often found little offerings under her bed. At other times, she noticed her pillow had a strange smell, and on investigating she found something scented under her mattress. She knew what was happening. They had asked a *dukun*—a shaman—to try to influence her feelings.

All these incidents she recounted to Nyoman Astawa, her boyfriend.

"If we believe this stuff, it can affect us," Nyoman said. "But if we pay no attention, and if our hearts stay strong when we find these things, then they can do us no harm."

"But I'm frightened, darling. Even though we don't believe in all this, we're still Balinese."

"True, Tini, we're Balinese. But you must realize that the Godhead, Ida Sang Hyang Widi Wasa, is higher and more powerful than any black magic. We must pray to strengthen our beliefs. There's no other way. We can oppose evil with our own hearts. And our heart's strength will come as a blessing from God. Ida Sang Hyang Widi Wasa will help us."

As the days went by, Tini was more and more aware that all her relatives had turned against her. She was on her own except for Nyoman Astawa, and he came less frequently to her house once her aunt had warned him directly not to pester Ida Ayu Ketut Sumartini. Since then they'd had to meet elsewhere.

The house where she boarded now turned into a kind of frightening cage, where she always felt anxious and suspicious. She never felt at peace there. Sometimes she was afraid even to go into her own room. It seemed as if evil spirits lay in wait for her there. Once that sort of feeling took hold of her, the hairs on the back of her neck would stand on end as she stood in the doorway. She would quickly back away, then go to the kitchen and drink a glass of sugar water, as Nyoman had told her to do. Then she'd spend a few minutes calming herself by reading in the lounge room. Or she'd keep busy playing cassettes. Only when she'd calmed down would she go to her room. Once, she'd lifted up her mattress, and found nothing. She'd checked underneath it, and opened the cupboard. There was nothing out of the ordinary. Then as her eyes scoured the room, she saw a small wrapped object hanging by the door-frame. Her heart beat fast; she broke into a sweat. She could see that the package was made of plain cloth, and as she gazed at it, her aunt had suddenly appeared.

"That just came from Bali. Don't touch it. For safety's sake," her aunt warned her, immediately on the defensive.

"And look," she went on, "They've sent these two silver bracelets. They're pretty, aren't they? Just right for your wrist. One's for you and the other's for me. Such lovely gifts are meant to be worn."

Pretending to do it lovingly, her aunt fastened the bracelet on her right wrist, and wore the other one herself. She noticed her aunt's lips murmuring a prayer.

"I don't like wearing bracelets," Tini muttered.

"Oh, but you must. See how pretty it makes your hand look. You really should wear it. All the family wish for your wellbeing."

Tini hated it. Somehow she controlled her anger. But she couldn't hold back her tears. She broke down sobbing.

"I feel so weak." She moved aside and lay down, her mind full of confusion.

"That's a sign that you've been put under a spell. That fellow has had magic worked on you," her aunt said and went away in disgust, leaving her alone in her room. Tini wept. She covered her mouth and put her pillow over her head. She felt full of bitterness, as though her wounds had been splashed with vinegar.

News of what had happened that day soon reached Bali. And from Bali another package was sent a few days later.

"You must keep this in your bra," her aunt said. Have it with you all the time." Tini took the white package and held it close to her breast. Then she left the house to go to the university. Her thoughts had been troubled since the night before, when she'd been aware that her aunt had cautiously entered her room and fanned a cloth, as though she were chasing off mosquitoes. A few drops of water had fallen on Tini's face, but she kept her eyes closed as though she were asleep. After that, she lay awake the whole night long. Feelings of fear, irritation, insult, a desire to rebel, and all sorts of other emotions were mixed together so that her mind was unable to rest.

That day, she didn't attend lectures. From a public telephone booth she arranged a meeting with her boyfriend, and at two o'clock she went to his house. There they agreed to open the package that had just arrived. Stitch by stitch they undid it, and found it contained several needles, five grains of rice, herbs, thread, cotton, and some other objects with something scribbled on them.

"So this stuff is what you're so afraid of, Tini," said Nyoman Astawa. "Centuries ago, in the days of Majapahit or Jayaprana, it would have been natural for us to be frightened. But not now. Why should we be afraid? Objects like these have no power so long as we don't give them any. This is just trash. Don't you think we should just burn it?" Nyoman Astawa tried to curb his anger, but he couldn't conceal it. His eyes grew bigger, and the tiny red veins in his eyeballs inflamed as he held his breath. Tini was acutely conscious of all this.

"What do you think, Nyoman?"

"Let's burn it."

"But I'm still afraid," Tini said. She stopped Nyoman's hand as he started to light a match.

"Why?" The glint in his eyes shone into Tim's eyes and she felt his courage ignite her own.

"The *dukun* will find out."

"How could he? He's far away in Bali. Only God will know." He struck the match and this time Tini's hand didn't restrain him. The contents of the package in the ashtray were soon consumed by flames. Nyoman Astawa watched them burning and glanced occasionally at his girlfriend's face. In her eyes he could see a shadow of fear.

"Look, Tini—it's all turned to ashes now, except for the needles."

They held hands tightly, then put their arms around each other. Presently they refilled the pouch with cotton from a drawer.

In spite of all this, however, the couple was finally forced to split up. Tini's entire extended family agreed that she must move back to Bali. This was the only way they could hope to save the family's reputation. Her mother came from Bali to fetch her, and Tini was forced to return with her.

Before the two lovers were separated, they managed to go to the temple to pray together and make vows to each other before the gods. They took a packet of flowers and incense and prayed to Ida Sang Hyang Widi Wasa that a way might be opened for their love.

"God is far more powerful than the *dukun,* Tini," Nyoman said. "A pure heart can never be overcome by evil. Make your heart strong until our time comes."

Now all that was behind her, and in the bus, Tini finally fell asleep.

In the half light of dawn, her mother woke and looked long at the face of her daughter.

At five o'clock, just as the eastern sky was turning a glorious red, the bus arrived at their house. The mother woke her daughter; they got down and found several people waiting for them. But Tini was shocked when she was forbidden to enter the house compound because the person preparing the offerings for their arrival wasn't quite ready. She was astonished. She had never imagined that something like this would happen. She was overcome by a wave of hatred, and wept bitterly.

"Be patient, Dayu Tut. We are all praying for your safety."

Tini didn't know whose voice had spoken from among the crowd. She could only cry, and she covered her face with her hands. In the meantime, the offerings had been brought out, and she followed the instructions of her grandmother, who conducted the proceedings.

She couldn't forgive what her family was doing. She felt deeply humiliated. The ceremony greeting her was one used specially for someone who had just escaped from some danger, such as recovering after a period in hospital, or having been involved in a near-fatal accident. A ceremony, in fact, for people saved from the jaws of death. Her boyfriend had been equated with a danger to overcomemenace.

Her heart screamed in protest, but she could do nothing to oppose all this. Nothing but weep. At the height of her grief, she no longer knew what was happening. She collapsed, overwhelmed, and lost consciousness.

Her relatives were in turmoil. The *dukun* was called, and Tini regained consciousness to hear him muttering at her side. She swore and she cursed, yet not a word escaped her lips.

During those first days in Bali, she argued incessantly with her mother, Dayu Biang. It didn't make sense to her that her older brother had been allowed to marry a girl of lower caste, while she, as a woman of high Brahman caste, found her wish to marry a man of lower caste constantly thwarted. And for what reason? Especially in these more progressive times.

"A man can raise the rank of his wife if she's from a lower caste," her mother said. "The woman becomes part of our family. But with you, it would be the opposite. You'd lose your rank with a low-caste man. You'd be dragged down. Wouldn't you feel ashamed? We would."

"But that isn't fair," said Tini. "God created us equal at birth."

"You're Balinese! Not a Muslim or Christian."

"Oh, it's all so old-fashioned!" She tried to walk away. But her mother held her arm. "What did you say?"

"These traditional customs about caste that you wrap me in. They're too restrictive for me now that I've grown up. If they're forced on me, they'll rip apart and leave me naked."

"So this is the result of you going away to school?"

Wounds to the heart never heal. After spending several months with her family, Tini still didn't feel at peace. There had been no chance to correspond with Nyoman Astawa, but she constantly kept in her mind the promises they'd made at the temple in Jakarta. Although she was unhappy, she tried to hide it by taking part in all the family's activities. And so her family came to believe, as the *dukun* said, that Tini had broken up with Nyoman Astawa. She was never prevented from going to the movies or other diversions. In fact, all her wishes were fulfilled by her family, and finally, she came to be well liked by all her relatives.

Then one day at the hairdresser's, by chance, she ran into an old friend from her school days in Bali. Mery took her home to her house near the market. Afterwards Tini often visited her, and thanks to Mery's help she began communicating with Nyoman Astawa again.

The festival of Galungan kept all Balinese Hindus busy, and Ida Ayu Ketut Sumartini was no exception. She was occupied just like any other Balinese woman. In the early morning she was ready to go to the family temple, carrying offerings on her head. She prayed in all sincerity. The family watched her happily, although they couldn't be certain exactly what she was murmuring. They didn't realize that she was making use of this opportunity to pray not only for the protection of the gods and her ancestors, but also to say a silent farewell and to ask for forgiveness. Sadness made her blood run hot for a moment as she realized that she was leaving behind what she'd loved since she was a little girl. She looked around her at the shrines in the family temple, at the world in which she had been born and raised, and which she must now leave behind. Sweet memories haunted her mind, the crowds in the temple at her tooth-filing ceremony, the day her father had died and his cremation.

"Oh my gods and ancestors, forgive your servant," she prayed. "I will continue to worship you from afar. I am leaving soon, and will be despised if I come back here to worship you. Oh gods and ancestors, I know you will hear when I call you no matter where I am..."

In the evening there was an *arja* drama performance in the community hall. She watched for only a short time, and then went back to her bedroom. She began to feel uncertain.

"Am I strong enough to leave this house behind? Do I have the strength to drag myself even further away from the love of my family? Is it true that happiness awaits me when I arrive there?" She tossed and turned, unable to sleep, listening to the distant sounds of the gamelan and the laughter of the audience. Toward morning she drifted into a brief uneasy sleep.

She told her mother merely that she was off to Mery's. And so she left.

But when her mother heard a visitor calling from the front gate after sunset, Ida Ayu Ketut Sumartini still had not returned home. Her mother had begun to inquire about her daughter from the neighbors during the afternoon. But it never passed through her mind that that evening, the day after Galungan, she would receive visitors like this.

"Is anyone at home?" the visitors called again, and she hurried to open the gate. Three men in traditional dress were waiting there, and Dayu Biang's heart almost burst at the sight of these unexpected guests. She gathered all her strength to face them; but once their purpose was made clear to her, she fainted. The men had been sent by Nyoman Astawa's family to inform her that Ida Ayu Ketut Sumartini had run off with her boyfriend and they were going to get married. The family was thrown into a state of shock. One of them went off to find the *dukun* who had been involved. But unfortunately he had not returned home since Galungan, and was still at a gambling place.

At the moment when the sun slipped down to the foot of the mountains, a plane was taking off at Ngurah Rai airport. The red rays were becoming fainter, leaving remnants of gold at the edges of the black clouds hanging over the island of Bali.

"Look, Tini, we are going to fly straight through those black rain clouds. Look down there at paradise laid out in all its beauty." The two of them contemplated the view from the plane's window.

The Garuda Airlines plane soared up, passing through the banks of black clouds that sullied the Balinese sky, and the clouds parted like a black cloth split by some sharp, foreign object.

Once the plane was above them, the clouds, like cotton wool, closed over again and prevented the couple looking down from seeing, below them, the island known as paradise.

Ketut Sumartini whispered in her heart, "I will love you from afar." She nestled her head on her boyfriend's shoulder.

The Bag

The drumbeat from the mosque and the call to the sunset prayer had just faded into the march of time. The stillness brought on the night, covering a fragment of the face of life like a black veil masking the face of woman. And the thin line of cloud, brushed by the light of the setting sun, was swept aside. The prison clinic's patients were now back inside their cell, each one stretched out in his own allotted space, lined up like sardines in a can. Sometimes a few words of conversation would break the silence. Somewhere in the background someone was reciting a bedtime prayer, asking God that they might all awake to the new day with the hope of ongoing life.

Hope!

They didn't regard anything as strange any more. It was all just normal. They were like passengers waiting for a train to arrive—a train that would bring either recovery or death. A train that didn't run to any timetable.

It was a different matter with Bawa, one of the prisoners who helped out in the clinic. As he walked around the prison yard he seemed to be counting his footsteps. With his head bent forward, he picked his way through the rows of vegetables. Occasionally he'd look up into the darkening sky, as if he were searching for something.

"I'm sure she won't come," he muttered definitively to himself. He kept on repeating the same words, trying to smother the hope that was tormenting him. "No, she won't be here tomorrow. But what's happened?"

The question made the waves of anxiety inside him rise to new heights. He was like a little boat in the middle of the ocean, far from land, with sea and sky uniting to form a boundary line that blocked his view of the future. He couldn't break through it, whichever way he turned, and there were no compass points to show him which way to go. The sea beneath him rose and fell to the rhythm of his anxiety, a restlessness that never left him.

There was a struggle going on inside him. He was trying to make reason prevail over his emotions, to make reason the guiding light that would see him through what was left of his life. That was why he did his best to crush the hope of seeing Lia whenever it surfaced in his emotions. It involved a huge amount of effort, because it was precisely when he was feeling powerless like this that he really needed something from her. A bag from Lia. But he had seen the boundary line, and he didn't want to climb a mountain of false hopes, just to be tipped head over heels and plunged back into the depths of his reality.

"She won't be coming anymore! No more! Not even her bag!" He let out a silent scream. He gritted his teeth and clenched his fists. It was as if he were setting off a bomb to blow up any seeds of hope that might be growing inside him.

"No. She won't be coming anymore!" The drum announcing the night prayer brought him up sharp. Then came the voice of the muezzin, calling a halt to his inner struggle. What a noble sound it was, so rhythmic, so sharp, like a knife cutting through the web obstructing his view of the future. It quivered and reverberated in the air around him, lifting him up into the heavens, into empty space, into the deep wells of an imagined life that brought him ultimately into a state of submission. Submission to the will of God!

That state of submission calmed his restless anxiety in a way nothing else could. He was flooded by a sense of peace like a gentle rain quenching the heat of day, a feeling of emptiness cutting through the torments that racked his being, a strength that wrapped itself around him and eased the never-ending effort to keep his life going. He stood still, leaning against the old casuarina tree beside the well so he wouldn't be seen by the prison officer looking in from the front of the yard. He wasn't a Muslim, but he delighted in the sound of the call to prayer. He could feel all the meaning that was distilled in the sound and the rhythm, as it summoned him into the cell block to rest, until the call to the dawn prayer opened the door on a new day.

The night crept on. He lay there wide awake, trying out all the ways he knew of falling asleep. He counted his breaths. A thousand breaths, but sleep seemed to be even further out of reach. He squeezed his eyes tightly shut, but the images of all he'd lived through just grew sharper in his head. The first real pleasure he'd had during the trials of life in this place had been one afternoon when one of the officers who dealt with food parcels for the prisoners in his block had handed him a green bag.

"Bawa, would you like a parcel?" officer Parman had teased him.

"For me?" It took him a few moments to be able to ask the question.

"Yes."

"Who's it from?" He hurried towards his cellmate who'd taken delivery of the travel bag at the entrance to the block. All his cellmates gathered around, watching the look on his face. He struggled to contain the tears welling up in his eyes.

"Something from home?" asked someone beside him.

"I don't know. It doesn't say who it's from."

"But it must be for you. There's no other Bawa here." He could almost smell the skin of the person who'd filled the bag with food.

He went into the cell block and took out everything in the bag. His cellmates stood by him.

"Something from your wife, Bawa?" one of them asked.

He didn't dare reply, because he didn't know how. It was only wives and other family members who were permitted to send the prisoners food, and Lia wasn't a relative and wasn't yet his wife. But she'd had the courage to send him this bag.

From that day on, his status in the prison changed. From being someone on the receiving end of handouts, now he was the one passing gifts around. From being someone invited to share in a meal, now he was inviting one of his cellmates who never received any parcels to join him in a meal.

"That bag means such a lot," he told himself that night. He wondered whether she had done it out of a general concern for other people, or because she loved him. Is there a gulf separating courage and love, financial means and love? At last he fell asleep. He dreamt of meeting up with Lia and saying to her, "Lia, whatever motivated you to send that bag, I can tell you that just by being here you've given me reason to live... that bag is you!"

In the days leading up to this event, he'd often talked about the matter of food parcels with others who never received them, even though they all had wives. Some of them interpreted it as a sign that they were no longer loved. Others were able to see it from a broader perspective, as just another indication of lives full of hardship.

"That bag says a lot. It isn't just a source of food; there are lots of other meanings hidden inside it." From that day on, his beloved Lia sent him a food parcel every ten days.

So from that moment, he lived in hope and expectation of the next bag arriving. It came to have great significance for him, and for a number of others as well. It was always a feast, with rice, meat, milk, sugar, dried food, or noodles of various kinds. Sometimes in the bag he found a couple of long strands of hair.

"She must have sent me these hairs on purpose. They're long hairs, so maybe she's been letting her hair grow, just as I suggested," Bawa thought happily.

Then came a national holiday when he got to see her in person. Their first meeting lasted half an hour, but to Bawa it was all over in a flash. Half an hour was nothing after a year's separation with no news passing between them. There was so much to say, so many stories laden with all they'd endured since the time they were parted.

"Bawa, be sure to share that food with your friends. Don't worry about anything except staying well."

"That's all we have time for, Lia. There's still so much I want to know about what's been happening to you, but the time's up. Look after yourself. I don't know when I'll be home again."

After that they saw each other regularly. But every time they met there was always something new about her. It was now clear to him that his beloved girl had grown up. There was a new integrity shining in her eyes, a yearning that was full of enthusiasm for life.

"I used to be afraid to come. It's taken me all this time to get over it. I'm sorry, I let you suffer here alone too long."

"There's nothing to be sorry about, Lia. We learn from whatever life has in store for us."

Lia didn't cry. She was like a mother with a sick child, hiding her own concerns to build up the strength he needed to survive. The touch of their fingertips through a gap in the wire mesh that separated them was like an electric cable joining two live currents that flowed out of bodies so thoroughly separated: one in the free and open air outside and the other hemmed in on the inside.

"Where do you get the money to send me so much food?"

"Believe me, Bawa, I earn it all respectably. After work hours I help out in a medical practice. Sometimes I take care of private patients."

"You must be worn out from working so hard."

"It doesn't matter as long as I can do something for you."

Their fingertips gripped each other through the wire. Their eyes formed a golden bridge.

"Where did you put my present, Lia?"

"I hung it above my bed. I look at it all the time. Have you learned to make carvings now?"

"For you I feel as if I could do anything. Do you like it?"

"Yes, I do."

They smiled at each other. Bawa had sent her a number of carvings he'd made out of coconut shells. One of them was a carving of two birds, one inside a cage and the other perched on top of it.

After that, he heard from one of his friends who worked in the office that dealt with incoming parcels that Lia hadn't been bringing the bag herself. She had been giving it to one of the prisoner's wives to bring it in for her. Bawa immediately assumed that Lia was working a morning shift and wasn't able to come herself. There was not the slightest change in the contents of the bag, and it was only on her next visit that Bawa could see that she had been ill. She was pale and thin, but her smile tried to hide what she'd been through.

"I'm better now. I've got my strength back."

"Don't try to force things. You really must watch your health. If you need to miss a delivery, I'll understand." He paused a moment, and then said, "I can't leave you anything of value."

Lia bowed her head as he spoke.

"I know this is very hard on you. You don't need to ask anyone's advice. Just think carefully, and when you've decided what you want to do, stick to it."

"Don't start thinking silly things, Bawa."

Now her eyes were like windows splashed with rain. She quickly looked down and wiped them with her handkerchief.

"No, Lia. I trust you. That's why I'm telling you to do whatever's best for you. You should take your age into account. Remember, I don't know when I'll get out of here."

Bawa knew his beloved well, he knew her limits. This was the only way he could give something to her, he thought. Their meeting had made him so sad this time. His girl's face looked long and thin, her skin pale and lifeless. Her dull dry hair was piled up on her head, revealing the neck he'd so admired, not just long and slender, but with the graceful curve of the areca nut palm.

"What's happening to you, Lia? Tell me. You must stay well. There's something wrong. What is it? Tell me."

"Yes, Bawa."

Before she had a chance to say anything more, a whistle sounded to mark the end of visiting hours. He wanted to kiss her, but the wire mesh separating them made it impossible.

He pressed her fingertips. They were cold and damp. She looked straight at him, and Bawa could still see the flicker of fire in her eyes. They smiled at each other as a guard touched Bawa on the shoulder.

"Keep it for next time," the guard said.

When visiting hours were over it was usual for the prisoners to tell each other their news. As soon as Bawa got back to the cell block, his close friends gathered around him.

"How is your girl? Prettier than ever?" Digdo ventured.

"What's the news?" asked Imam.

"She's been sick. She's lost weight."

"Yes, the poor thing. This is all too much for her."

"So what did you say?"

"I told her to do what's best for her."

"Marry someone else?" Imam seemed to leap on what he'd said.

Before Bawa had a chance to reply, someone else jumped in: "It's always the same. It's so hard to find someone who'll be faithful.

You're weird. Did you really tell her to go off and get married? Who's going to send you food parcels now?"

"Just a moment. I haven't told you the full story yet," Bawa shot back. Then he told them all about their meeting.

"You are weird, you know," Imam said. "You seem to think you're above it all, that you don't need anyone to bring you things to eat. If she does go off and leave you, you'll go back to eating what they hand out in here. Do you expect someone else to share with you? It wouldn't bother you to see someone else's family running around trying to find the money to send food parcels? All because you've gone and told Lia to stop sending them to you? We need to increase the number of families sending food in. Not reduce it. Weird. I can't understand the way you think." Imam babbled on uncontrollably.

"I didn't tell her to go and marry someone else. All I did was suggest that she should do what's best for her own life."

"Bawa, aren't you listening? Everyone else here is asking their families to keep waiting for them to come home, and if at all possible to keep bringing food parcels. You're doing the opposite. You should be saying, 'Lia, wait for me. I need your food parcels. Don't leave me.' And something else, Bawa. Everyone here quietly admires your girl for coming here when things are so tough. A girl who keeps her promise in good times, you can find anywhere. Look at what you've got! You're not even married yet and she does all this for you. How will it be after you're married? She'll be fantastic. You can introduce me to her when we get out of here Bawa. I envy you."

Bawa didn't reply. He was upset, but he kept it to himself, because he knew that even though Imam was a close friend, his thinking was really limited. He waited until the situation had calmed down before seeming to make a joke of it, saying, "Hey, Imam, untangle your brains and they might be just long enough to hold up your underpants!"

"Ah, bullshit! Just what you'd expect from a weirdo artist!" They laughed, and the others joined in, diffusing the tension that hung in the air.

"But, Imam, Lia does have the right to make her own decisions. Why is it that we are always telling people we love freedom and all that sort of stuff, but when it comes to people we care about we act like tyrants? Love is giving, not making demands. Affection is taking responsibility, not pretty words. And love and affection bring risks that we have to face up to, not burdens we need to get rid of. If you're going to take a bath you've got to be prepared to get wet."

"There you go, off on your high horse again. Moralizing away in your ivory tower. Just you wait and see. If Lia really does stop sending you food parcels, I bet you'll end up a bit wacko, just like the guys whose wives have gone off and married someone else."

"Have you ever turned things around? What would you do if it was your wife in here and you were on the outside?"

No one said a word. Bawa went on twisting the knife.

"We're always thinking about ourselves. We make demands on other people, expecting them to shoulder our burdens. We look at everything from the point of view of our interests, not the interests of others, even though they might be the wives we used to sleep with every night. They're only human after all, with their own limitations. They have rights. They're not just our appendages. Those bags they give us with the food in them keep us alive, but who gives us the right to demand them? No one!"

"OK, you're smarter than me when it comes to talking. But talk is like food. Talking is easy, it's the shitting that's hard."

After that last meeting, Lisa's food parcels had kept on coming in the usual way. But now it was almost a month since he'd seen that green bag. When at first it didn't turn up, Imam would often tease Bawa about it, but as time went on he, too, began to share the general sense of gloom.

Time stretched out like a piece of string being unraveled from its spool. But something kept making its presence felt in the growing expanse before him, like the sound of a piano being played in a silent room in the deepening night. He didn't know where it was coming from, but he could hear it very clearly. And he knew that the sound of the piano was Lia's voice: "Father disapproves of our relationship."

"Yes, I guessed as much. It's because of the shape of my eyes, even though our skin color is almost the same, and your mother was one of my people."

"But my brother is on our side. Without my knowledge, it turns out he's been talking to Father about it in letters."

"This just isn't fair, Lia. My people have always regarded yours as an older brother. They think that if a woman from this older brother's family marries a man of my people, it's just not right. But the other way round it's not a problem. So what did you say?"

"I told Father he was out of touch."

"You dared say that to him?"

"I did. And he didn't say anything."

"But that doesn't mean he accepted it. Tell him that you have to make your own choices and do what you know is right and true for yourself."

"I'll say that if he brings it up again."

Bawa lay awake the whole night.

"What has happened to her? Did she get married? Is she ill? Has she been arrested?" There were no answers. The next day he still hoped he might see her, because it was a scheduled meeting day. He was on edge from early in the morning, watching anyone who happened to be carrying a bag that looked like hers. The tension in his body was tearing him apart, and his eyes were shining wildly. He went back and forth to the latrines, but each time he could only pass a few drops of cold urine. Suddenly, he felt tired. He looked about for something to do, just to get his mind off what was happening. The sun was climbing higher and higher in the sky. He kept walking up and down until finally the bell rang to signal the end of visiting hours and parcel deliveries. Lia hadn't come. His disappointment struck him down like a knife going through his flesh. His emotions tore his reason to shreds, as the bitter truth cut its way inside him. How great was the distance between reason and emotion, between reality and hope, between individual human beings and humanity itself.

Rumors suggested that on the outside the situation was becoming critical, and economic conditions were causing more and more hardship. This added to Bawa's anxiety.

That night, Imam came up and spoke to him, "That's the risk, Bawa," he said bluntly. But then he went on, "I'd just like to know what happened to your girl. I didn't think I'd see you left for another man, like what happened to me. Maybe she's sick. Maybe she's gone back to the village. Let's hope everything's OK."

Bawa didn't reply. He just sat there, gazing into the distance.

They did what they could to find out what had happened to Lia. In the end, it turned out that one of the prisoners lived not far from where Lia worked. He promised to tell his wife to go there and ask about her.

A few weeks later Imam had some news for Bawa.

"Stay calm, now."

"She's married? I've prepared myself for the worst. Just tell me. This has gone beyond a joke."

"Don't get the wrong idea. She's still true to you. Easy does it, now. The enemy's not at the gates yet."

"Stop teasing me. Come on, out with it." The urgency in Bawa's voice was serious.

"The news isn't as bad as it could be. Lia's working overseas. That's as much as I know. It's not clear where she is or what she's doing."

"I understand. This is just the opening chapter of a long story that's going to end in an absence in my life. I'm prepared for the loss, and I did tell her to do what was best for her. Maybe this is the best thing for her."

"There's more than one fish in the sea, Bawa. Don't give up hope. But think of that green bag."

"There was something in that bag that I'm not likely to find in anyone else, or anyone else's bag."

"What?"

Bawa didn't reply. He just looked away and wiped his eyes.

Luh Galuh

She had plenty of time this morning to contemplate the rice barn. Bright sunlight gilded the eastern side of the roof. The old corrugated iron sheeting clearly showed its deterioration —like her own face, where brown spots and wrinkles had replaced freshness and inner glow. She was seated on the steps of her house, at first intending to think about what kind of work she could do that day. But the shape of the rice barn had suddenly caught her eye. Its plank walls were full of holes, consumed by age and termites. When she passed underneath she was often sprinkled from above by a fine wood powder.

Yes, it was on that platform of neatly bound bamboo slats that she once played market games with her friends. There she would arrange offerings, and on holidays her father would prepare special ceremonial dishes. Several times the white screen of the shadow play had been erected there for a performance, and the place had often been used for playing cards. Now it was covered with chicken droppings and a thick layer of dust. Some of the flattened bamboo slats had broken and never been replaced. Only the six pillars that held up the belly of the rice barn were still strong, untouched by termites.

The rice barn resembled a raised pavilion. In the old days when there were festivities she used to sleep there, because the rooms and verandah of the main house were filled with guests and the supplies for making offerings. There, people were crammed in, but underneath the rice barn were only the sprawling pigs. Their endless snorting was like a lullaby. When her mother wanted to get rice from inside the storeroom, she was not allowed to climb up alongside her in case she fell. Worse, she might disturb the goddess Sri, who ruled over the bundles of unhusked rice that filled the barn.

But that was long ago. So long ago! Now the rice barn was like an old worn-out basket, full of rat holes; nothing important ever took place there. Everything had passed on, including her fame as an *arja* dancer.

Apparently it had been of little use for her parents to carry out the *telu bulanan*, the naming ceremony for a three-month-old baby, where they decided to call her Luh Sekarwati. It was her grandmother who came up with the name Sekar, meaning Flower. In the baby's round face, her bright eyes with their thick brows and dark lashes against her creamy skin were like flower buds emerging from dense undergrowth. But 'Sekarwati' had only ever appeared on her school report card, as it turned out. For the most part she was known as Luh Galuh, after the role of the princess she performed in the *arja* plays, in which she hypnotized her audiences. She did not reject the name Luh Galuh, and a wave of pride filled her heart at the praise implied.

This was Luh Galuh, who like many other simple people was not able to control the course of her life. She had been dissolved, diverted, dragged, discarded, and dumped, with no choice on her part. Choosing was a luxury she had never been able to afford.

Something was eating at her from within. She scratched at her sides, her fingers probing the bones of her ribcage as if rubbing the bamboo slats of the pavilion. She scratched again and again but found not one louse or ant. The itchy feeling then moved to her calves. With dexterity she scratched the lumpy flesh hanging from dry bones covered with creased and scaly skin. Her scratching fingers probed down further, to the bony knobs of her ankles. She scratched repeatedly until her nails etched white lines, and still she scratched, until the white lines cut through her skin and the cuts began to sting. She spit into her hand and rubbed the spit into the cuts. Her scratching then spread further downward, right to the soles of her feet. They were swollen, filled with fluid that her body could not dispose of as sweat or urine. Carefully she stroked her feet; every night she coated them with a paste of ground rice and roots that now formed a dry, cracked crust. She ruefully regarded their condition. Ever since her feet became swollen, she had felt she needed all her strength just to walk. Frustration clouded her eyes. The jobs she did all required great strength. Even worse, work was being snatched away from her by the strange machines that had suddenly appeared.

Still her eyes were focused on the rice barn. She could pick out the shape of the wooden mortar, like a prow abandoned by a fisherman, turned upside down. The mortar, which had always sung out the rice husking music with the rhythm of the striking pestle, was now just the remains of a part of life overtaken by progress. So, too, were the two stone mortars implanted in the ground, still stretching open their mouths that had not chewed unhulled rice for a long time. The mortar had always meant so much to Luh Galuh. For years she had made a living from it, as long as she was strong enough to work as a rice huller. Almost every day there were customers asking her to pound their rice. From this service she earned not only wages in the form of rice, but also the chaff from the husking. Few people in the village were as trusted as Luh Galuh, because she had never cheated anyone on their share of her labor. She hulled people's rice in her own mortar, away from the customer's house.

At one time she had worked in the village as a harvester during the rice harvest. But now many fields had been turned into

buildings, or tennis courts, or bus terminals. And so she had lost
her means of support. She had tried to follow the example of Madé
Siti and become a construction laborer, but that had only lasted a
few months. She couldn't compete with the younger, livelier, more
agile laborers.

Even so, there were still people who owned rice fields in the
village, so that rice-husking work still offered opportunity—at
least until the hulling machines stole her livelihood. People now
preferred to send their sheaves to the mechanical huller, because it
was faster, cheaper, and more efficient. Now the only work left for
somebody like Luh Galuh was to fetch and carry the harvested rice
and hulled grain between the owner's home and the huller. And
such work could not be expected to be continuous. Because of this,
she had steeled herself to borrow some money from her nephew
to sell vegetables in front of her house. Many people bought, but
there was little income, and most of that went to paying off her
debt. She could manage for only three months, and then her small
capital was used up. When she could not pay back her nephew's
money, their relationship had soured. Actually, she had three
brothers and a dozen nephews, all of whom were working. One
was a doctor in Java, and several had good positions outside or
within her own district. But her hopes of receiving help from any
of them came to nothing. For a while she was a domestic servant.
She had always relied on her own strength to make a living. She
once had a husband, but he disappeared without a word in the
mid-1960s, during that period when people, as if possessed, killed
other people for not sharing the same opinion. Since she no longer
had a husband, she had returned to her parents and lived in their
home—a rare generosity on their part. And once both her parents
had died, she lived alone without the slightest bit of inheritance.
Her parents' possessions and rice fields went entirely to her brothers.
She became aware of what it meant to be born a woman. Now, she
was only a visitor in the family home—nothing more!

Her feet started to swell up after she was invited by her oldest brother to the city, to prepare the ritual offerings for the tooth-filing of his third child. It had taken nearly ten days. Day and night she worked hard to make all the preparations. At such moments she was really useful, and there was no one in the family to compare with her. She was not only hard-working, she knew everything about the art of offerings. People praised her work, and did not know whom to consult if she was not present. But it was at those times, only those times, that she meant anything! So she returned home dragging her heavy feet, back aching. She had been provided with money for bus fare, enough rice for three or four days, and some of the leftover food from the ceremonial feast. From her nephew she had received a second-hand length of batik, and a screen-printed T-shirt that was faded and worn. Quite a gift to repay such a debt of honor!

Even time itself passes heedless of the wishes of the powerless. People like Luh Galuh of course might have desires, but the endlessly passing days never took notice. The days raced by, glancing at her with one eye, then turning their faces away. They didn't care!

Luh Galuh rose from her seat. Only she knew for certain what stirred inside her. She took a basket from the kitchen hearth, which had been without a fire all morning. Then, wanting to descend the step, she pulled her sarong up to her knees. Her right hand crept along the pillar, seeking a hold. Her left hand held the edge of the basket perched on her head. Her joints trembled, supporting her leaning body, as with greatest care she moved the palm of her right hand from the pillar to her right knee, which was still bent, so that she would not fall over as she stepped onto her left foot. After standing up, she grimaced with the pain in her ankles, rubbing her side, painfully stiff. Then she moved, swaying, each step tentative, until she reached the front gate, on the edge of the public road.

Cars and motorcycles crowded the street. This was something new, which had cost increasingly more lives over the past few years. Of course things were easier—to go to the beach now it was no longer necessary to walk three kilometers. You could take a public *bemo* that passed by every five minutes or so. Same thing for going down to the river, or if you wanted to get to the post office or the marketplace. Fifty rupiah would get you there, and in fact for fifty rupiah you could get to any place within the city or its outskirts.

This was the reason the horse-carriage drivers were getting more fresh air than passenger fares. There were fewer of them, too. For going up to the hills there were plenty of motorcycles; you didn't need to walk anymore. At night, too, people no longer had to bother with flashlights; electricity brightened their homes. The road, which used to be so muddy, now shone with its layer of asphalt, though there were pot-holes here and there. The old pushcarts employed to transport the harvest had long since been retired and now were eaten by termites alongside the houses of their owners. The small stalls people had run in the village had gone out of business; instead, pickup trucks full of wares passed by several times a day, offering everything from shrimp paste to lipstick. They were mobile shops, and you could pay for your purchases on credit. Women seemed to think it more important to buy lipstick than toothbrushes, and to enjoy the taste of packaged seasoning more than a piece of salt fish.

She stood erect on the threshold of the gate. Her dull eyes probed the scene as if re-acquainting herself with her own neighborhood. So much had disappeared. The trees along the road. Women and their daughters crowding around the public faucet getting water. The gamelan group at the community hall. Nowadays, people's friendliness lacked sincerity, and the leafy shade had disappeared.

Despite the ease and convenience offered by the passing transportation, Luh Galuh—thinking of Nyoman Madri down on the riverbank—began to move her feet step by step. She had no money for a *bemo* fare, and she certainly wasn't daring enough to walk on the smooth pavement of the street. The motor vehicles shooting by were the supreme rulers of the public road. Pedestrians had to move to the side and skirt the rocky edge of the drainage ditch. Even there you might not be safe. If two trucks passed each other on the road, pedestrians had to jump to the far side of the ditch. As she went along taking her careful steps, she thought about abandoning her plan to meet up with Nyoman Madri, who supported herself by carrying sand from the river up to the main road. She realized such labor was too much for her limited strength. But what was she to do?

As she hesitated, her eyes alighted on two young men. They had just crossed the road and were approaching her. There was no chance to think before they arrived in front of her.

"Auntie Luh, here's a visitor who wants to photograph you," said a brown-skinned youth, introducing the tourist with him.

"Ah, I'm so old and disgusting. It's embarrassing," she said instantly. She covered her face with the end of the towel hanging from her shoulders. But the tourist, without waiting for permission, had already shot several pictures, up close and at a distance.

"It's OK, no problem," said the visitor in halting Indonesian.

"I'm so embarrassed," she hissed again. She let go of the towel and let him photograph her as much as he cared to.

"Who are you?" Luh Galuh asked the young man with brown skin.

"I'm Ketut Mendra Patih's son."

"Oh, you're so grown up," and her hand moved to touch his arm.

Ketut Mendra Patih had been one of her friends from the *arja*. The name *patih* had stuck to him because in the drama he played the *patih*, chief minister to the king. Then the brown-skinned youth quickly explained to his guest who Luh Galuh had been in her youth. The tourist nodded his head up and down like a chicken pecking grain.

Speaking in English to the youth, the visitor said he would like to interview Luh Galuh the next day. When Luh Galuh was told of the plan, she nodded, too. Her nostrils flared. The light of her eyes, for years obscured by sadness, suddenly shone forth like rays of sunset from the gaps in a dark sky.

"Ask him for a little money for Auntie." Her face turned from one to the other. The three of them were quiet, as if something was stuck in their throats. Finally, the tourist groped in his pockes and presented a five-hundred rupiah note to Luh Galuh.

"Thank you, sir."

"Don't forget about tomorrow," he replied.

Luh Galuh moved with a lighter step. The image of the visitor took shape in her mind, and her feelings soared. Tomorrow, early in the morning, she would prepare herself with the best clothes she had.

And who could say just why the visitor was so drawn to Luh Galuh? That sharp-eyed tourist was like an animal that had found its prey. Without wasting a moment, he took possession of Luh Galuh's image. The tourist thought of how wonderful a picture he had taken—a Balinese woman, dirty, scrawny, once a famous dancer, still displaying the power to fight for life, with her basket on her head, her skirt hitched up to her knees, with her swollen feet, wearing that old T-shirt with the printed message: 'Paradise'.

Luh Galuh kept on walking, but her feelings now were mixed. She was ashamed, proud, awkward, timid, and perturbed all at once. After a moment, she looked back. The two men were climbing into a *bemo*. The *bemo* sped off as if scoffing at her, belching exhaust from its tailpipe. And Luh Galuh kept on walking.

Bridge of Light

Lubang Buaya, the Crocodile Hole: it's the first time in my life I've set foot in this place. It feels like I'm walking on air, hardly daring to let my feet touch the ground. Ever since I got off the bus and entered the grounds, I've been conscious of every step, enveloped in my own solitude. It's not as though I'm alone here: there are people everywhere, walking in all directions. They go past me or walk with me, turning away or going on ahead of me. I have no expectation of meeting anyone I've ever known, and no desire to let anyone impinge on my sense of solitude.

I walk on, making my own path across the open field, following the depths and direction of my own thoughts. I stop to look at the well that gives this place its name, and I steal a glance at the caged reliefs, through the spaces between the bars. Then, following my instincts, I head off in a different direction. Finally I find myself standing in front of the statues of the Heroes of the Revolution, with the sun bearing down on me from an empty sky.

"Generals, do you agree with what is on display here?"

No one steps forward to answer my question. I don't give up. I ask again, "Generals, is what I see here what really happened to you?"

Not a word, not a whisper. Not even the sound of air passing someone's lips. I am entirely alone.

All of a sudden the hairs rise on my skin. I take hold of myself, stand up straight and rub my eyes. The statues are still there, lined up in full military splendor. None of them has moved, there hasn't been a breath of smoke, a flicker of flame or a drop of dew. Nothing. And I am still fully conscious. I move my fingers. Everything is functioning normally. But the hairs on my skin still stand on end, and the pores seem to enlarge. The heat of the sun is beginning to draw out the sweat.

"Something did happen," I whisper. I stand still, looking intently at each of the statues in turn. But still there is no answer to my question.

"Generals, I can only feel pity for you if what you experienced was different from what this place is telling me happened to you. I pity you if they are using you and manipulating what happened to serve up lies to our children."

The words don't pass my lips. If I were to speak, my voice would most certainly be nothing more than a hoarse and broken stammer. High emotion seems to run through my whole body, like a fine electric current.

Suddenly I hear the voice of a woman standing in the middle of a crowd of schoolchildren. I hadn't been aware of the primary school excursion group standing around the reliefs and casting occasional glances at the statues of the generals. A few uniformed guides are with them; some of them carry cameras. But there is another group as well, who seem to be making a film. I direct my gaze to the woman with them. She is white-haired and also white-skinned, with grey-blue eyes. And she is speaking to the children, in a loud, clear voice. "This is all untrue, children. There were no women dancing around naked. Nobody gouged out the generals' eyes and nobody cut off their genitals. That's all lies." The children stand mesmerized by the old lady with white skin. She's leaning on a stick, firmly planted on the ground to give her some support.

"That was a brave thing to do," I whisper.

"Don't talk to the children that way, ma'am," says one of the uniformed female guides, going up to her.

But she keeps on saying that the depictions in the reliefs are lies. "This is a falsification of history. This is all lies," she says firmly.

Several of the guides, both male and female, appear unsure how to handle the situation and are motioning to each other.

"You must not talk like that in front of schoolchildren," says the woman in uniform. One of the guides moves away.

"I have historical proof of what I am saying. I myself suffered imprisonment because of this slander." And on she goes, drawing attention to aspects of the reliefs that are not true. More of the guides crowd around her and try to send the children away. But the children are transfixed.

Finally, this white-haired and white-skinned old woman is asked to report to the office of the commander of the Lubang Buaya security guard. Some hours later, she and her group depart the area.

There is something I am still searching for. Something I've never been able to find. I've read the Cornell University white paper on the 1965 coup; I've seen the film which reveals the autopsy report on the way the generals died; I've seen the film we all have to watch about the events; and I've read many books about it. But I've never been in direct dialogue with those heroes of the revolution themselves, the generals whose statues are revered every October first.

I start walking again, exploring the far reaches of the Lubang Buaya grounds. There are crowds of people here, sheltering from the sun in the shade of the trees. I sit for a while on the steps of a pavilion, then I retrace my steps. But still I find nothing, because I have no idea what it is I'm looking for. Truth? The facts? Blame? Lies or deceit? Imagination?

The sun inclines towards the west and the heat of the day begins to ease. As the passing of the seconds seems to quicken pace, I intensify the hunt for this thing I cannot name.

The crowds start to thin out, and the breeze blows leaves from the trees as dusk begins to fall. I'm getting closer and closer to the exit, knowing I've failed to find whatever it is I'm looking for. I'm the last one here, I think to myself. But suddenly there is a woman walking beside me. She smiles and I smile back.

"Good afternoon."

"Good afternoon."

"Just leaving?"

"Yes, I'm going home."

"I've been watching you since early afternoon. You've been looking for something here."

"Oh, no. I'm not looking for anything."

"Tell the truth," she says gently.

The security police are on to me, I think. I don't know myself what I am doing here, and she just accused me of looking for something. Careful! My instincts spark a warning signal.

"No, it's nothing. I'm just looking around. I haven't been here before."

"But you are looking for something, and you haven't found it. Where are you going to look now?"

"No, no." I avoid the question, keeping my expression unchanged so I don't show any sign of fear. It's been such a long time I've been carrying around this suspicion of anyone I don't know, always thinking everyone is working for the security police.

"I'm looking for something, too, something I can't find either." She has a reassuring effect on me, this woman who's easy to talk to, slim, dressed in white and with the odd grey hair starting to show. But still, it's possible this is all part of her technique.

"What is it you're looking for?" I say.

"Something. I don't know. I've looked everywhere but I can't find it."

"Strange."

"Just like yourself. But it's really not strange, is it? Let's sit for a while. There, under that tree." She leads the way and I follow. I'm falling into her trap.

I feel as though I've touched the ground. Sitting here on a bench outside the Lubang Buaya grounds.

"We won't find the truth in there." She points inside the gates.

"No."

"There are a lot of puzzles."

"Yes."

"I felt disappointed."

Yes."

"People go on about who is right and who is wrong."

"Yes."

"There are lots of people who think their side was victimized."

"Yes."

"Are you a victim?"

"No."

"Do you feel those generals are your enemies?"

"No."

"So who is your enemy?"

I don't say anything. This is a trick question.

"Why are you silent?"

"I'm exercising my right to say nothing."

"Perhaps we both have the same enemy."

"Maybe, maybe not."

"I know who you are. But you don't know me."

"No, I don't. Who are you?"

"My father was one of those heroes of the revolution."

"Really? But you look so… so ordinary! How did you get here?"

"I came on the bus."

"Like me."

"So what are you doing here? Is it a place of pilgrimage?"

"I don't know."

"Like me."

"You're looking for the truth, aren't you?"

"Yes."

"You want to set the record straight, don't you?"

"No."

"So you accept the version of our nation's history that exists now?"

"No. I want our history to be like what they say in the Fuji film ad, as varied in color as the original."

"So it's not a matter of correcting history?"

"No, it's democratizing history."

"That's just playing with words."

"So be it then."

"You'd like to tear down those statues and those reliefs, wouldn't you?"

"No. I'd like to put up a new set of reliefs beside them."

"That amounts to the same thing."

"Maybe."

"It's getting late. We'd better move on, or the security guard will be arresting us."

We stand up and start walking. Smiling to each other. When we reach the road we start talking again. I speak first.

"Do you feel proud to be the daughter of one of the heroes of the revolution?"

"No, I don't."

I stare at her in amazement, trying to read the light in her eyes, a light that seems to come from deep within her.

"Do you feel proud to be one of the victims?"

"I'm not a victim. I'm a survivor."

"Very well. Does that make you feel proud?"

"Yes, it does."

She watches me intently, looking for a spark of light in my eyes.

"What is it you are looking for?" I say.

"The facts. Not who's right and who's wrong. That's not healthy."

Suddenly she starts walking, not saying anything. I run after her and ask, "Where are you going?"

"I'm going to trace the path of history from this place to home."

I stand still and watch her, till she disappears from view.

Wounded Longing

My first meeting with Mémé Mokoh had to be held somewhere other than at home. It seems that everyone was of the opinion that the time was "not yet right", and I didn't dare argue. Apparently, my older brother, who held an important position in the government at the time of the mass slaughter of communists, was afraid of the consequences if I were to come straight home. As I learned later, he had discussed my return with a number of other leading figures in our village—the village chief and the leaders of organizations for young people—and all had said the time was "not yet right". This is why my meeting with Mémé Mokoh took place in S.

I traveled overland, from S to J, while Mémé Mokoh and the rest of her party—my two older and my two younger siblings and my Aunt Kerti—came by ferry across the strait to meet me.

Mémé Mokoh, who couldn't walk because of her broken hip, was very pleased to see me in the small hotel where we were all staying. She and her group had arrived first, because their bus got in at three in the morning, whereas my train didn't arrive until ten. I was met at the station by someone who was like a brother to me, a police officer who used to stay with us when he was at school in our town. Mémé Mokoh didn't cry when we met. She looked at me with eyes that shone with the sparks of longing and affection. I hugged her, and she said nothing at all. She patted my shoulder and stroked my head.

"Where have you been all this time?"

"In Jakarta, in jail."

"Everyone said you were dead, but I didn't believe them. I wouldn't let them hold a cremation ceremony for you. There was one stupid priest who said you'd been killed, far away from home."

"How are you?" I asked. "Are you well?"

"Yes. It's just that I can't walk. Can you make me better?"

"Yes, I can help you to heal."

"That's wonderful. When will you be able to come home?"

"I can come right now," I answered lightly.

"No," my brother cut in quickly. "We're working out when's the best time. The situation isn't completely safe at the moment."

Mémé wiped the tears streaming down her face.

"Don't worry," I told her. "I'll be coming home soon."

I knew exactly what my brother meant. He was in an awkward position. I was on the list of those who were to be killed—that's what my brother-in-law had told me—but here I was, still alive. My younger brother, on the other hand, was marked out not for death but for imprisonment. He, however, had managed to escape to Java, also thanks to my older brother and some of his close friends. So we were both still alive, whereas other people who'd been on the list of those to be killed had indeed met death at the butchers' hands, even though the time of slaughter was now over.

According to my brother-in-law, who had also escaped death, my older brother had also managed to save the lives of several other relatives and neighbors, people who hadn't played a prominent political role prior to the September 30 incident. In return for his kindness, he often received gifts of rice and other produce at harvest time.

That first meeting provided me with a lot of information, including the political map of my village and the names of the people who had been killed. Fifteen of my fellow villagers had died. Surprisingly, Putu Sarka, whose house had served as the local office of the Indonesian Communist Party, had survived the initial wave of killing. He had taken refuge at the office of social affairs, and he was not on any of the lists of those who were taken away each night. But when the time of slaughter was declared over, he was told to go home by the officer who was making arrangements for the people who had fled to the social affairs office. The next day he went home. Before he reached his home, he was told to report to the army commander, who had set up his office in the local meeting hall. He went to the meeting hall and stood before the commander.

"Actually, you were on the death list," said the commander.

Putu Sarka was silent. His eyes blinked as he looked at the commander, and then he bowed his head.

"So what do you want now?" said the officer standing next to the commander, his broad-bladed sword hanging from his waist.

Putu Sarka remained silent. He wasn't able to make a decision about his own fate.

"Your friends are all dead. You're the only one left. Now, do you want to live, or die?"

Putu Sarka raised his head. A wave of fear shot through him at the news that all his friends had been killed. Calmly he replied that if he was to be killed, then so be it.

"Of course, because you were on the list."

"Very well, but let me first say farewell to my wife and child."

"You won't find them at your place any more. They've gone back to your wife's family."

"Take me there, then."

Three men accompanied him. He sat down at his brother-in-law's food stall and asked for a glass of coffee. They asked his wife to come outside and bring their three-year-old child. After taking a sip of coffee, he got up and approached his wife, who was holding the child against her chest.

"They're going to kill me. I've come to say good-bye. Take good care of our child."

Their eyes met. His wife said nothing, but tears ran down her cheeks. She was afraid to say anything, afraid to cry. The child cried, and she covered its mouth. The commander's eyes bore into her like fire.

"That's enough. Go inside now," he ordered.

Putu Sarka turned away. One of the men accompanying him tied his thumbs together behind his back. They took him to the graveyard, where an executioner finished him off in front of a crowd of onlookers.

My brother-in-law told me who the executioners in my village had been. I knew them all. One was one of my classmates in primary school, another was a boy who was good at martial arts and was known for his arrogance and taste for a fight. There were also a few who, in order to save their own skins, were prepared to kill their own comrades.

On the second night in S, my brother asked me to join him on the verandah in front of the hotel. The others were all in bed.

"I want to tell you something." His voice was restrained. I looked straight at him, as we sat side by side on a small bench. He was nearly whispering, and I did not say anything. I just waited for what he had to say. After a long pause, he went on.

"I'm sure you've wondered about what I did in 1965."

"Yes, I have. But I don't know anything about what really happened."

"The atmosphere in our village was tense. There'd been hostilities for a long time. If we hadn't acted, it would definitely have been us who were killed." He was silent. I too said nothing.

"People were saying that the Communist Youth League was killing people in N." He was silent again.

"So then what happened?"

"So then we cooperated with the army. We rounded up the people who they'd marked for killing and brought them to the meeting hall. Then, when the order came from somewhere, the killing started."

"You didn't protest?"

There was no reply.

"If they hadn't been killed then, they would have killed us, for sure. People said the communists had already prepared graves at the back of their houses and that they had a list of people they were going to kill. We heard they found the list in the home of I Ketut's house, the Communist Youth leader."

"Who found it?"

"The army."

I kept quiet and studied his lifeless face. His body seemed to be flowing with hot lava, making him edgy.

"Mémé told me not to get blood on my hands," he said, hanging his head.

"But you yourself didn't take part in the killing?" I half-whispered.

"No. When I was told to cut off I Blonjor's head, I looked at him and his face suddenly changed into your face. I had my sword out, but I didn't have the strength to lift it. I backed down, and asked someone else to do it. I went home terrified that night, afraid they'd kill me because I wasn't able to do the job on I Blonjor."

It felt like being in a graveyard. Silent and still. Every now and then one of us slapped at a mosquito around our ears. Occasionally the sound of a bell on a passing *becak* broke the silence. A series of recurring images kept going through my mind: the village graveyard; the face of I Blonjor, one of my classmates in third grade at primary school; the face of I Ngancok, who my brother-in-law had described as a cold-blooded executioner. He said that he would often lick the blood off his sword after decapitating someone.

"Who actually led the extermination action?" I asked very cautiously.

"We always reported to the officials. And we received our information from them, too. But people in the village made lists as well, names of people who should die. There were only a few of them, but later it got out of control, and there was no way of stopping it. Everyone was naming other people who should be killed. A lot of people took action of their own accord. Some committed rapes, and we punished them. We killed the rapists, because they were defiling our cause." My brother seemed enthused by the memory.

"And then?" I asked more boldly.

"We had to put a stop to it. Former soldiers in the revolution against the Dutch were being killed by young kids who didn't know anything about them. They knew nothing of their service to the country, and just went ahead and executed them without our knowledge. It was all out of some kind of resentment, some frustrated sense of hatred. We finally had to put an end to it. If we hadn't…"

"Did the army agree that the killing should be stopped?"

"Yes, they allowed it to stop. Even though there were still the odd one or two being killed. Not everyone obeyed orders."

That night I couldn't sleep. Not a wink. I no longer wanted to go back home. I felt nervous and afraid.

"Was my brother making a confession?" I couldn't speak for thinking about it. My longing to be reunited with my family suddenly felt as though someone had cut through it with a sharp knife, leaving a bleeding wound in its place. I closed my eyes and turned over on my stomach. My eyes burned with tears. Who was he? Who was my brother?

On the last night in the hotel, my brother again asked me to join him on the verandah. I felt very awkward with him. His story had wounded me, and I still felt the pain. I could not hold back my tears. I wiped them away, but my nose was still runny. My brother sat still for a long time before he spoke.

"We ended up in the same boat," suddenly his voice came from nowhere.

"What do you mean, the same?" My voice sounded like I had knocked into a wall.

"They've been after me, too. Right up till now. My loyalty to the nation and my belief in the national ideology are under question, and it's impossible for me to get a promotion."

"Why?"

"Since 1971, I've opposed the government party. These days, that's enough to make a person an enemy of the state."

He Wept in Front of the TV

People called him Wayah Dalang, "Grandfather Puppeteer". He wasn't really a *dalang*, but he was so good at telling stories the name had seemed to suit him. His tales of evil spirits battling it out as thunderbolts, black clouds, and lightning flashes in the skies above Sanur beach were legendary. His hands would fly back and forth like a *dalang* manipulating the puppets, the same as when he would captivate an audience with the story of how he had once tricked a Dutch soldier by hiding behind a single banana leaf out in a village somewhere. People would fall about laughing over his jokes, but his digs at other people sometimes made them angry. When he was off on one of his stories he would quite often pass a derogatory remark about anyone who flashed into his head. He was one of several men in the village who were highly regarded for the role they had played in the war of independence. He was an accomplished martial arts practitioner and he could also perform masked dances. So the name Wayah Dalang had stuck, right into his eighties.

The sound of the bamboos brushing against each other beside his house was the background music to his life. Trees of all kinds gave him shelter from the sun, just as his bushy eyebrows shaded his eyes. When it rained, the narrow track that led to the house became muddy and slippery. And it was at one of those times that Wayah Dalang emerged from his bedroom to greet Madé Rata, who had made her way through the mud to visit him. He was bent over into a shape that resembled the letter C, not just because of the ravages of age but more because he'd been a carpenter for most of his life, bent over planing planks of wood for hours on end, day in and day out.

All the friends of his youth, even some of those younger than himself, had now departed this life. His much younger wife, seventeen years his junior, and three sons from among his eight children had also passed away.

"How much longer must I watch my children die?" he asked his guest. "Why doesn't the great Ida Sanghyang Widi call me to heaven?"

"Come now, Wayah. Don't be like that. We still need you here with us," Madé Rata replied. She was a distant relative of his grandchildren's generation, now the director of a bank in another town; but whenever she returned home to the village she would always make a point of paying a visit to Wayah Dalang, bringing him some granulated sugar or other things to eat. Now and again she'd give him a new shirt or a bit of money.

"Whenever I think of your grandmother, I have the feeling I've never done enough to repay all that I owe her."

"But you risked your life for this country. You were a great revolutionary fighter. You're a veteran of the revolution."

"Your grandmother did a lot for the revolution as well. She sheltered the young fighters in your home and made sure they had enough to eat whenever they came down out of the mountains. When the war ended and we were free, those young men still often got together at your grandmother's house. And she never forgot me, either. Whatever she had, she would call me in and share it. It might be rice ready for planting or rice for cooking, food of all kinds.

"Why didn't you stay in the army, like Wayah Sarka?"

"I didn't get through the selection process. It was hard to get in, and I failed because I couldn't read and write."

Wayah Dalang laughed, and it sounded like he was laughing at himself. "How could someone like me pass that kind of test? I went to school up in the jungle. When I came down from the mountains, I looked for work everywhere, but there was nothing. So I ended up a carpenter, and in the end I couldn't stand up straight anymore."

Madé Ratna made some tea, and Wayah Dalang's bent back moved over the table as he picked up his cup. Madé Ratna watched in silence, as though she was reliving the pain he had felt at his failure to join the army.

"But you're still an army veteran," she said after a while.

Wayah Dalang didn't reply. He turned the conversation to his son the policeman, who, one day right out of the blue, had been dismissed from the force.

"Can you do something to help I Budi? He was fired from the police force. Now he sits around with nothing to do, just the occasional odd job as a stone mason."

"I'll do what I can. But there are no jobs for regular employees at the moment."

"That's all right. You know, he's the only one of my children who got to senior high school, and now he's just a stone mason."

"I'll do what I can," Madé Ratna repeated before taking her leave. All through the conversation she'd had to speak up, because Wayah Dalang had now lost his hearing in one ear. His eyesight was still sharp, because he'd had a cataract operation that a number of people had helped pay for. The kindness of his grandchildren's generation sometimes reduced him to tears. Whether they were the children of his own family or more distant relatives like Madé Ratna, it made no difference.

But it was when he was watching television that his tears would flow most freely. His little set with its fourteen-inch screen sat in the cramped living room, where space was restricted because of the bamboo platforms that were used for preparing offerings. There were two low chairs and a table of indeterminate color, and on the walls hung a few photos of Wayah Dalang as a young man just down from the mountains and as a veteran wearing the characteristic yellow hat. Photos of his wife, his children and grandchildren, were scattered about the walls as well. Wayah Dalang lived there with two of his sons and their families. They ran a stall in the market and made a bit of extra money doing odd jobs.

Wayah Dalang sat in front of the TV set with his head leaning forward on the end of his C-shaped back. No one else was home. His grandchildren had left earlier than usual for school, their uniforms clean and pressed for the flag raising ceremony. It was the anniversary of Indonesian Independence Day.

"You know, don't you, that here in our village five heroes of the revolution fell to Dutch bullets?" Wayah Dalang said one evening in the house of one of his friends who'd passed away. The friend had been part of the group who'd gone up into the mountains in a tactical retreat during the war against the Dutch, and Wayah Dalang was ready to begin one of his stories.

"I Madé Tirta was killed in Seririt during a shoot-out in the market. The Dutch were trying to move up into the mountains, but the young revolutionary fighters were there to block their way. That's where Madé Tirta fell, and one of his friends who survived brought back his ring as proof of his death. I Nyoman Moong was shot in the village of Panjir, taken by surprise as he was setting off for the mountains early one morning. He left behind a pregnant wife. There were lots of spies around Panjir. I Ketut Lanus was shot in the village temple. The Dutch soldiers came on him out in the fields and chased him back towards the village. He was trying to climb the walls of the temple when he was hit.

"How many is that?" he asked one of the people listening.

"Three, Wayah. Who were the other two?"

"One of them was shot during an exchange of fire in Pabean. He was a captain, Captain Jasa. A real daredevil, but the Dutch outsmarted him."

"How come, Wayah?"

"You couldn't engage the Dutch in open conflict. You had to use guerrilla tactics. That's how I survived."

"Who was the other one, Wayah?"

"Well, that one was a really brave fighter, but he didn't know how to behave himself. He used all kinds of charms to protect himself from the bullets, but he molested a lot of women. He had a wife in nearly every village he passed through."

"So how did he die?"

"Executed by his own commander for disturbing public order."

"You said he used charms against the bullets," said someone from a corner of the room.

"The commander asked him to hand over the charms first."

No-one spoke. They seemed to be in a world they'd never read about or even heard of in school.

"You should go and pay your respects to them sometimes at Heroes Park. There's more to know about than just General Sudirman, Diponegoro, and the other national heroes. Our own village has its heroes."

Wayah Dalang was watching the flag raising ceremony on his little TV. The boys and girls in their white uniforms stood straight and tall, lined up in orderly rows in their different class groups. As the red and white flag began its ascent to the top of the pole, tears seeped from his eyes and ran down his cheeks. The strains of the national anthem seemed to be tugging at his heart strings.

"Gone. All gone. I'm waiting here to die," he sighed.

He seemed to travel back in time, back to the years of chaos. The years when the raucous cries of the crows spread fear in everyone's heart. The years when people went berserk.

He had been summoned in those days by one of the leading men in the village, someone he'd once shared time with in the jungle, waging guerrilla warfare. Back then, the man had been one of their commanders.

"I was never a member of the Communist Party, sir," he said in answer to his commander's question.

"Yes, we know that. But you did help them sometimes."

"Yes, I did. They were nephews of mine. Lots of them were in the Nationalist Party, lots in the Communist Party. They would come asking for my help, one after the other. I made flagpoles for them, helped carry their belongings when they moved house. When the communists held public events I was a security guard. When the nationalists put plays on I did the same for them. They were all nephews of mine, sir. I couldn't turn my nephews away."

"Well, to prove that you weren't a communist, now you have to help us."

"Yes, sir."

So from that day on, he had the job of removing the bodies lying in the dust beside Heroes Park and taking them to the village cemetery for burial. Sometimes he also had to tie the hands of people who were to be executed. Whatever they ordered him to do, he had no choice but to do it. But then one night he was told to join a group that was taking three young men to be executed. All three of them were communists who had fought with him in the mountains. He couldn't get out of it, because there were lots of others with him, so he kept his sorrow hidden away in his heart.

Several days later he fell ill; but even laboring under a fever he had to report to his commander to ask for sick leave. He went home and counted on his fingers the number of people in his community who'd been executed. From the western to the eastern end of the village there were fifteen of them.

On the TV screen veterans with their yellow hats and chests bedecked with medals sat together in rows of chairs. Wayah Dalang kept on wiping away his tears.

"Why do I have to look at this? Why can't I just die and be done with it?"

One year after that time of uncontrolled violence, he'd received a letter from the Office of Veterans' Affairs telling him that his status as a veteran was to be withdrawn because he was regarded as "tainted" by communism.

He lifted up his C-shaped body and hobbled off to his bedroom. There he took down from the top of the wardrobe the faded hat he'd worn as a guerrilla fighter. He put it on and lay his bent frame down on the bed. And all the while the bamboos kept brushing together, sounding out the background music to his life.

Letter of Invitation

It was around four in the afternoon. There was a knock on the door and my wife went to see who was there. I heard a man's voice asking if I was home. I heard her reply, yes, I was here. She asked him to take a seat and then called out to me that someone wanted to see me.

I came out of the bedroom and saw someone I didn't know, seated in my living room and smiling in my direction. With him were two men. One was Pak Marjan, the leader of the neighborhood association in an adjacent ward and the head of security in the next level of the local administration. The other was Pak Memet, the head of the neighborhood association in my area.

"I came along because our guest here thought he might have trouble finding the house," said Pak Marjan as if to explain his presence.

Without any word of introduction, the visitor handed me a stenciled sheet of paper, A-4 in size. "I've come here to deliver this letter of invitation."

I skimmed the document, already knowing its spirit and intent. The words themselves were not important. They could be lies with the same kind of duplicitousness that marked the character of my visitor. I had enough experience to understand the difference between the ostensible meaning of words on a page and the inner meaning they contained.

"Can I bring a few things with me?" I asked evenly.

"No need. You won't be gone long," my visitor replied.

"I'll just get changed, in that case. I can't go like this." I was wearing an undershirt and an old pair of crumpled and faded trousers. Without waiting for his reply, I went back into the bedroom and changed into a long sleeved shirt and t-shirt, with socks and clean underpants, and put a clean handkerchief in my pocket. I took everything else out of my pockets, other than a few small denomination notes. I left my identity card as well, in case it got lost somewhere along the way, or at my destination.

"Should I bring this?" I asked my escort, pointing to the letter of invitation.

"Yes, bring it so they know what this is about," he replied.

I said goodbye to my wife, standing there with our four-month old baby on her hip. The color had gone out of her face and her eyes were empty. I kissed her forehead.

"It's all right," I told her. "Don't worry."

My visitor, Pak Marjan, and Pak Memet took leave of her together. When we came out into the front yard, it turned out there were three other men with them. One had just appeared from the entrance to the alleyway beside my house, another was there outside the house itself, and a third came running up from the end of the street in front. Apparently they'd dispersed to cover as much ground as possible. One of them then started up the patrol van, and asked me to take a seat on the middle bench, flanked by two of the others.

"Where are we going?" I asked the man in charge. There was no address on the letter of invitation.

"You'll find out," was all he said.

I kept quiet, recognizing the streets we were taking.

His answer epitomized the culture and form of civilization he embodied. It implied his position and my position within it, as well as its broader social institutions. It was a form of civilization and culture that had been operating for decades in this country, with a full set of state and civil institutions. There were public prosecutors.

There was a high court. There was a police force. There were civil institutions that were said to act in the interests of the people. There were pages and pages of statutes purporting to protect people, but in practice just making fools of them. His answer said it all. Finally we reached our destination. I was ushered into an empty room.

"Wait here," one of my escorts ordered.

Doing as I was told, I sat down on a chair in the empty room. There were three tables, each of them with a chair placed on either side on them. My watch showed 4:35, the same time indicated by the clock on the wall. I heard the sound of footsteps in the adjoining room. The sound of many footsteps. But no voices. Neither was there any suggestion of a radio or TV. Occasionally I could hear the noise of a vehicle entering or leaving the compound. Suddenly the sound of laughter broke the silence. It was coming from quite far away, certainly not from the room next door. The light swinging from the ceiling wasn't on. The seconds turned into minutes, the minutes into hours, and I just stayed sitting there. No one came. The sound of footsteps had ceased. The sound of vehicles as well. No more laughter either. I covered an ear with my hand, and could hear the sound of my heartbeats, coming fast and loud.

There was no other sound at all. Silence gripped the air. But then came the noise of bustling footsteps. Followed by a voice organizing a line of soldiers. Then a command. Then the sound of army boots. And all the while I stayed sitting alone in an empty room. I didn't want to look at my watch. My body was wet with perspiration. There was no air conditioner, no fan in operation. Darkness fell, adding to the silence.

Sitting there by myself, my thoughts wandered to the students at Flinders University, who'd welcomed me into their midst when I was visiting Adelaide in South Australia. I thought of the friends I'd made when I was in Melbourne. There'd been a party outdoors one night, and I'd trodden on dry leaves as the moon seemed to open both its arms in a warm and welcoming embrace. The blue skies

and fresh winds of autumn. I remembered the researcher who'd
received me in Canberra, inviting me to stay at her house. Her
daughter played the violin, and I listened with rapt attention. A
journalist who'd spent time in Indonesia gave me accommodation
in Sydney. When she went to work, I looked after the daughter
she'd had with a Vietnamese man. I saw, too, the dark grimy
faces of the Harijans, the untouchables of Madras I'd instructed
in acupressure. I remembered the landless farmer in Koita south
of Dhaka in Bangladesh, where I'd spent a few days for theatre
workshops. I'd helped treat his swollen knee with acupuncture. I
remembered a Singaporean friend who'd been detained after coming
back from Bangladesh, and a theater worker from the Philippines
who'd been met at the airport and was never heard of again. I saw
again the faces of my classmates from different countries in Berlin.
We'd gone along to classical music concerts together, and joined
in the dismantling of the Berlin Wall. Bare trees, a naked moon
and the midnight cold had filled me with an energy I'd never felt
at home, the chill in the air a source of refreshment for my weary
body. Freedom. I could feel again the irritation I'd felt at the way
people behaved in Taiwan and Hong Kong. I hadn't enjoyed myself
in either of those places. I thought of the well-known Malaysian
writer who'd been so friendly to me, sitting next to me during a
discussion of the book I wasn't able to publish in my own country.
I saw the face of the friend in Amsterdam who'd given me a lift
on her pushbike one drizzly night to visit one of her friends, a
"boat person". Images formed in my mind of the shop fronts in
Hamburg and Amsterdam where the sex workers were on display,
with smiles on their lips but maybe pain in their hearts. And lots
of other memories that came crowding into my head while I sat
there waiting in that empty room in the growing darkness. What
had brought them to life in the silence of that lonely room? Were
they all watching what I was doing there? I kept on swallowing to
assuage my thirst.

Suddenly a man entered the room. He switched on the light.

"Good evening, sir." I spoke first.

The man didn't reply. He pulled up a chair and sat down in front of me. He felt for something around his waist inside his shirt and placed a gun on the table.

"It's Bagus, right? If you were to die here, Bagus, it wouldn't mean a thing." His voice shot through me like a bayonet going into my heart.

I nodded.

"The principles of our national ideology don't apply here." His voice was like an explosion.

I nodded, more from shock than anything else.

"You might call this a blitzkrieg." He spoke again. As I watched, the spittle around his lips turned into blood.

I nodded again, leaning back.

"What can I do for you?" I asked slowly and politely, taking a deep breath. I thought of the way the phrase was used in English.

"You're not here to lecture me!" His voice shattered the night with the same force as his fist hitting the table. I was startled, but I stayed calmly sitting in my chair. His yelling was like a dog barking in my ears. My eyes held him central to my gaze, watching as his hefty safari-suited body began to turn into a guard dog. His teeth seemed to lengthen, and a snout seemed to form around his chin. I wiped my eyes, but when I looked again it was still there. He talked on and on, but it wasn't the sound of a human voice any more. I rubbed my ears, but all I could hear was the barking of a dog.

"What's happening? Why has he changed?" I wondered. Moments later came the sound of footsteps. How many, and whether they were people or animals, I didn't know any more.

From that night on, I was in a zoo with no cages. When I went to sleep I had rats crawling all over my body. Sometimes when I lost consciousness they nibbled at my fingers and tasted my blood. I fought martial arts battles with mosquitoes coming from nowhere in the dark. Cockroaches wandered all over me. Sometimes in the middle of the night there'd be a snake biting me, making me twist and turn as I gasped for breath and coughed uncontrollably. The snake bites would leave a stinging pain and poison coursing through my whole body, till I would writhe around in a frenzy with the sound of dogs howling in my ears. I could feel leeches sucking my blood. I couldn't tell any more what were dogs, what were snakes, what were cockroaches, leeches and rats. Sometimes they all came together, sometimes by themselves, ransacking every part of my body, from my backbone, my skull, my senses, to the hair on my head and my finger- and toenails.

After almost two weeks of this, the doors opened and I was free to go. The dogs, rats and cockroaches, the mosquitoes, leeches and ants had finished probing around in my body, smelling my sweat, my snot, my urine and saliva, even tasting my blood. All in search of the demon that was believed to have seeped into my body, infecting all my bodily organs and flowing in my blood, my sperm, my glands with such force that it had been able to carry me away, flying me around the world. The character and actions of that demon had violated all the rules of security, and it had broken out of the circles of barbed wire that were layered over all the islands of my homeland. They had been seeking the demon of communism in me, but hadn't found anything. Because some of the demon's progeny had taken up residence on thrones set up inside their own heads, chuckling away to themselves while the mother demon kept on laying eggs in her nest in the national parliament.

I stepped out of that small army compound into the larger one, with its layers of barbed wire raked across the islands of my homeland.

Nita

Nita sat down on the stairs leading up to the second floor, directly opposite where I was sitting at the end of the dining table. She had just arrived, but seeing me there in the dining room, she'd stopped and taken a seat on the stairs. The dining room adjoined the kitchen, where Uti, who helped around the house, was frying tempeh, her back turned towards us. The tempeh smelled good. Nita's hair was cut shoulder-length. It was thick and dark, and uncombed, it fell across her forehead. The color of lipstick still hovered about her lips, and eyeliner accentuated the edge of her lower eyelids. Whenever she spoke or smiled I could see a line of irregular and lusterless teeth. She took a deep breath and looked straight at me.

"I'd like to ask you something. Is that OK?" As she spoke, she kept moving her buttocks around on the step. She was wearing a calf-length pink skirt with a lively design of violet-colored flowers interspersed with green. It looked bright and cheerful. When she sat down, she had arranged the skirt so that her legs were tightly covered.

"Of course. What is it?"

"If I can just take a minute before the session begins…. It's like this. I've been having treatment everywhere, but nothing's had any effect."

"Where exactly have you been for treatment?"

"All over. In Bangkok, Kuala Lumpur, as well as Manado. And I've been to hospital here in Jakarta, too."

"You've been to Bangkok and Malaysia?" I asked, a note of surprise in my voice. She didn't reply straight away. She stood up.

"I just want to get something to drink."

She came towards the dining table, where there was a stoppered glass jar filled with a herbal medicinal powder. She measured out three teaspoonfuls, and mixed it with some hot water from the thermos and then cold water. A smile played about her lips.

"Excuse me while I take this," she said, returning to her place on the stairs.

"You've been to Bangkok and Kuala Lumpur? Well, how about that!" Uti threw in from the kitchen.

"Well, yes. Carried away by delusions of money. And on the wings of love." Nita burst out laughing, one hand over her mouth. Uti turned round and looked at her, breaking into a soundless laugh herself. She'd just turned off the stove and taken the fried tempeh out of the wok.

"The wings of love?" I asked.

"Right! Spoken as if you've never been in love yourself! Nothing can defeat the power of love. It's true, I went for love. Love is what made me human." Suddenly her voice slackened. She went quiet for a moment, as though something had taken hold of her. Then she wiped her eyes.

"So you're a world traveler? That's impressive!" I turned and looked at Uti. "How about you, Uti? Where have you been to?"

"Me? Just Garut to Jakarta. But not on the wings of love. An empty stomach, more likely!" We laughed together. Uti covered her mouth as she did so.

"This is how it's ended up," Nita said. "Love is always battling it out with hatred. Now it's hatred I'm dealing with. Often people see me as something less than human. They keep their distance, come out with abusive comments. As far as love's concerned, it's like it's evaporated off the surface of the earth for me."

Nita's voice seemed to stick in her throat. She brushed away the hair that hung down over her forehead and came to rest on her thick dark eyebrows. Underneath her hair, her complexion was clear. There was no trace of the blemishes of acne on her face, maybe because she'd had her skin carefully treated. When the laughter died down, she came out with another question, her voice frail and weak.

"What could it be, this thing I've got?"

"What are the symptoms?"

"I'm embarrassed; it sounds dirty to say it out loud," she said, "but I've got this hole in the skin behind my anus. Sometimes there's a clear discharge, or else it's thick, like puss. Sometimes there's blood too. So I can't sit for long. I have to lean on my side." She had been shifting the position of her buttocks all the time she'd been sitting there.

"Yes, any kind of wound in that area is very hard to cure, because the opening of the anus causes movement that stops it from healing. Especially in your case, what with you doing what you do…"

I was suddenly reminded of another woman, named Nelly, whom I had met in Makassar. In one of the meetings there, Nelly had told us about a friend of hers who used to put bricks out in the sun every day and then sit on them to treat her hemorrhoids, because she had no money to pay for medical treatment. But just as I was thinking of Nelly, Nita's voice brought me back to the present.

"Yes, I know…" was all she said, but I knew what she meant. I kept quiet, wanting to hear more of what she had to say.

Nita adjusted her sitting position, her breasts swinging in her loose-fitting t-shirt. The shadow of a black bra hovered inside the shirt.

"Are you still taking something for it? What doctor are you seeing?"

"I'm not doing anything now. I'm tired of it all, and the costs are astronomical. I just can't afford it."

"Is your anus sore? Have you had swelling there?"

"Yes, sometimes, especially when it gets a lot of use." Nita hid her face, bending over into her lap. Uti smiled at me with a look full of understanding, and I smiled back at her.

"If you don't have any prescription drugs, then take something herbal, like *sambiloto* for anti-inflammation, pain relief, and fever control. It also helps to clean the blood."

"You think my blood is dirty? she asked wide-eyed.

"I really don't know." I brushed her question aside, but then I went on, "You need *umbi dewa*, too, to help with the wound."

"One doctor said it was caused by silicon. I had silicon injections down here. Is there a connection?" she asked nonplussed as she stood to show off her spreading hips. She then laughed, as though having a laugh at herself. Uti laughed in return.

"What doctor told you that?"

"One in Kuala Lumpur when I was there getting treatment. I was really sick, with diarrhea, fever, and a cough that wouldn't go away."

"Where did you find out about your HIV status?"

"In Kuala Lumpur. When I wasn't getting any better they tested my blood."

"Did they give you any counseling before and after the test?"

"They did," Nita confirmed. "The doctor I had was very friendly. He told me about the risks of the test, and what I needed to do if the test was negative or positive." Her gaze was empty, hovering in the air between us. She was looking at me, but her eyes had lost their shine. She bowed her head and the light faded from her face.

"The doctor told me he was an HIV activist and he suggested that I join an AIDS-awareness organization so that I could speak to other people living with the disease. I learned a lot by doing that. One of the people said that HIV was like consumer capitalism which had infected the whole world and we were its victims. What do you think he meant by that?"

"You need to do a lot of reading, because the spread of HIV really is like consumer capitalism, there's a lot of politics involved. There's discrimination, stigmatization, the monopolies of the international drug companies, the issue of dependency on the advanced countries we call capitalist. It's a long story."

"I'd like to understand all that business. Have you got any books on it?"

"One of the books worth reading is *And the Band Played On*. And there are lots of doctors here like your doctor in Malaysia. Do you know Doctor Marya?"

"I've been to her clinic. She really is a good doctor, someone who looks out for transgender people. I once did a training program she organized. Wow, the data she has about transgender people! Can you believe it, one out of five are infected with HIV? Terrifying, really terrifying. The hair on the back of my neck was standing up."

The room suddenly went quiet. For a moment no-one spoke. The terms "HIV" and "AIDS" were like a gag in our mouths, leaving just our eyes to make the connection between us. They were like arms stretching out to clutch each other, drawing the three of us into a mutual embrace and giving warmth to the isolation each of us carried within us.

"Did you tell your boyfriend, when you found out you were positive?"

"He was already gone by then. My life fell apart after he left, because there was no love in it. That's why I said that love is a power

that has no equal. When I lost love, all I had was hatred, coming
at me from everywhere. Especially after my HIV status became
known."

"You didn't go back to your parents?"

·"Nah, I didn't want to be a burden to them," she said, "plus they
live a long way away."

"Where's that? Is that were you were born?"

"Yeah, in Yogya."

"Which part? I'm from Yogya myself."

"Way down south, in Kutoarjo." She smiled shyly.

"What's your CD4 count now?"

"Three hundred forty two," she said.

"You're not on anti-retrovirals?"

"No." She re-adjusted her sitting position.

"Can I ask you something a bit personal?"

"Sure, go ahead. I trust you."

"How did you come to be this way? Were you ever attracted to
women? Have you ever been married to a woman?"

"My parents pushed me in this direction from when I was just
a kid. Bought me lots of dolls, dressed me in girls' clothes, taught
me how to cook. Treated me just like a girl, in fact. But apart from
that, I did feel like I was a girl. It was only my physical body that
was male. And it wasn't anything I chose to be. When I went to
school, in primary and also junior high, I often wore my clothes
tight-fitting, like a girl. I took my pants and shirts in, so they'd hug
my body. When I was alone in my room, I'd often dress up and put
make-up on, the way girls do…"

"Didn't your parents tell you not to do it?"

"At first they did. But after a while, they let things be. They
realized how it was with me. And then when I grew up, my dad
gave me some words of warning: 'Don't go and destroy God's

handiwork. You must always keep your body just as God gave it to you'.

"I left home once I reached adulthood. I couldn't stand the ridicule, whether it was at school or out and about in the neighborhood. Later I found love. I met my boyfriend, the one who took me off to Bangkok and then died and left me all alone. I started to make a living for myself, in various ways. Then I moved to Malaysia and found out I was positive."

Nita's words flowed quickly, as though she was making her way across a fragile wooden bridge, placing her steps carefully even though she knew the bridge well. Hardship and danger seemed to have become a part of her.

"What about now? Are you still busking in the streets and cruising at night?"

"No, never. I'm living with my new partner now. And I'm on the staff of the organization. I'd like to be... what do you call it— one of those people who teach other people?"

"What would you like to teach?"

"All the things I've learned here. They're really useful for people like those of us living with the disease."

"Do you know Larasati?"

"The one in Batam? Yeah, I met her in Manila, at an HIV Congress. Wow, she was a real inspiration to me. A terrific person. She's got great self-confidence. She speaks great English, too. How come you know her?"

"I had long conversations with her when I was working as a facilitator in Batam. In the evenings, after class, we used to sit and chat in a restaurant, watching the flickering lights of Singapore in the distance. When I first saw her, I had no idea she was transgender. She was just like any pretty woman."

It was as though I were sitting in front of her now. She was wearing trousers and a fawn blazer over a white shirt. Her hair hung in waves that reached down to her shoulders. Her lipstick had a purplish tinge, and the line of her eyebrows was thick and dark. Her perfume wafted gently on the evening breeze. She didn't smoke.

"Sounds like you might have fallen in love with her!" Nita said quickly, her laughter tinkling through her words.

"I admired the clarity of her thinking. She used to say things along these lines: 'People like us suffer in many different ways. I have a woman's soul and a man's body. It's not something I wanted. Society can't accept the way I am, and demands that I adjust to its way of doing things. They refuse to accept anyone who has a different way of thinking and different beliefs. So I made myself someone who was legitimate in society's eyes, at the cost of being subjected to injustice. But now I don't care anymore. If they want to, they can call me a queer, a faggot, a pansy, I just don't care. This is who I am, and I'm not asking them for anything. I'm not some jobless person begging for food. I'm one of God's own authentic creations.' She cried when she told me what had happened at her hairdressing salon. 'One day, security men and health officials turned up out of the blue at our salon. They forced us to give them blood samples for testing. But they never came back to us with the results. So they made us scapegoats for the spread of HIV. And now, for those who are positive, things have gotten even worse. It's hard to get treatment, life is tough, and the ridicule and blame just goes on and on. You need a lot of guts to get on top of all this injustice.'"

A group of participants in the training program came in from the front room, heading up to the second floor. Nita stood up, but didn't go on ahead of them, standing aside instead to let them pass. Once they'd all gone she took a few more mouthfuls from her glass.

"Nita, how are you described on your ID card?" I managed to ask before she turned and went up the stairs.

"Male."

"What was your name?"

"Sunoto." She laughed softly as she climbed the stairs. Her smile was as wide as her swaying breasts. Then she poked out her tongue like a little girl, not at me, but at Uti who was waving to her. It was like a playful gesture to cover up all the sadness that was overwhelming her.

For some reason, the voice of Wayan Darma, a friend from my home village, sounded in my ears.

"As soon as you have anything to do with the bureaucracy in this country, you immediately become a second-class citizen." He was a political prisoner who was held for years without trial.

Eyes

I Wayan was a bit startled to see her already seated in 5C. Just a little while ago, she'd been right behind him in the line making its way from the boarding lounge to the air bridge. She'd even spoken to him, asking softly, "This is the plane for Medan, isn't it?" I Wayan had turned around to reply to the question and, as he did so, he found himself looking into a pair of eyes that seemed to roll right out from under her eyelids. Sparkling eyes. A moment later, they had retreated behind their wall of thick black eyelashes. But it was enough for him to catch the flash of light, an unspoken hello that caused his heart to skip a beat. It was just a flash, but it was fixed inside him. It broke open a store of memories he'd long kept hidden. They were the eyes of Nyoman Puri, the *tamulilingan* dancer.

When I Wayan came to a stop in front of her, she stood up and made room for him to take the seat beside her, 5B. I Wayan watched her out of the corner of his eye as she returned to flipping through the airline magazine. He organized himself, fastened his seat belt, and took out a book from the bag he'd put under the seat in front of him. He stopped paying her any attention, as she sat there with her head and neck swathed in a scarf that left a lock of hair resting on her forehead. She reminded him of the women who covered their heads and necks against the cold winds of autumn in Berlin.

The woman turned to him and asked, "Are you on your way home?"

I Wayan looked into her eyes. "No. I'm going to a seminar. Are you from Medan?"

"I live there, but I wasn't born there."

Feeling it was impolite to keep reading, I Wayan stuffed his book into the seat pocket.

The conversation began to flow like water gushing out of a cleft in the earth. I Wayan watched her eyes, because it was her eyes that did the talking. They danced about and kept him guessing. Sometimes they were like a pair of ballet dancers moving gracefully across a stage. Her nose was like the banks of a steep ravine that separated them, the nostrils ending in fine points above the curve of her lips. Her cheekbones were quite prominent, contributing to I Wayan's suspicion that her background was probably not all indigenous Indonesian. There had to be at least some Middle Eastern blood responsible for those facial features. But she had the same rounded dancing eyes of Nyoman Puri, his lost beloved. It was her nose and cheekbones that made the difference, sharper and more prominent than Nyoman Puri's had been.

Their conversation delved ever deeper into the recesses of their lives' journeys.

His interest piqued by the way she was wearing her scarf, I Wayan risked a mischievous enquiry. "Have you heard about the regional regulation that obliges women to wear the Islamic headdress?"

Her eyes flashed with anger. "Of course I've heard of it. The police even arrested me once when I went back to my village. I don't agree with it."

"You cover all of your head and your neck. Isn't it the same thing?"

"No. The way I wear my scarf is the way my grandmother covered her head. I do it because I don't want to catch cold. Look, my hair is showing. I like things to look natural. Not forced." Her hand touched the lock of hair hanging down over her forehead.

I Wayan remembered an article he'd once read. "Has it occurred to you that there might be some connection between this new trend for wearing headdresses and the garment industry?"

"Now you're teasing me," the woman said. "What, are you an economist, or a businessman?"

I Wayan just smiled in reply. Their conversation moved on to the way women covered their bodies in different cultures, before spilling over into issues like human trafficking, migrant workers, and a range of social inequalities.

"Did you hear about the candidate for district head somewhere who suggested that human trafficking was an issue for the department of trade?" Now I Wayan was trying to provoke a reaction.

"My God! You're not serious?"

"Could be."

They fell silent, each letting their thoughts roam free.

"What's your opinion about women who reveal nothing but their eyes?" the woman then asked.

Not stopping to think, I Wayan replied, "I don't think it's fair. They can see other people's bodies, but they keep their own bodies hidden."

His comment made them both want to laugh.

"Do women do it of their own free will, or because of rules men have made up to control them?" Now there was real fire in her eyes.

"Not by me, that's for sure," he said. "Maybe it's something men do in patriarchal contexts. Now let me ask you something. Do you think desire can be held in check by clothes that cover the whole body?"

"Your questions are getting close to the mark! No, of course not. The language of the body will always express itself no matter what. The neck can be tightly covered, but that very tightness can highlight its slender curve, and the effect can be very sexy. The eyes?

Yes, the eyes. What power anywhere can oblige a woman to cover her eyes? Or is it a matter of gouging her eyes out, so she can walk only with a white cane? No, clothes can't silence the language of the body and the whispers of desire. It all depends on what's going on in the mind."

"Gouging a woman's eyes out?" These words had caught I Wayan's attention.

"It's something I read about. Not gouging out the eyes of a woman, but the eyes of generals." Her tone was serious.

"Gouging out the eyes of generals?"

"I got it from my history teacher when I was in junior high."

"Did you believe him?"

"No, I didn't. It was a way of defaming women. There's a lot of information around now that tells a different story."

I Wayan stopped listening to what she was saying. He remembered the flashing eyes of Nyoman Puri when she danced the *tamulilingan*. He had fallen in love. He couldn't stop dreaming about those eyes. He painted pictures of them, wrote poems about them, till one day, his beloved Nyoman Puri was swallowed up in the savagery of early 1966. All because she had once performed a dance for a celebration of Indonesian Independence Day organized by the local branch of the communist youth league. It made no difference that she was part of the dance troupe in the presidential palaces in Bali and Jakarta.

"You've gone quiet. Who are you thinking about?" The voice of the woman beside him brought him back to the present.

"Oh yes, yes. I was thinking of someone whose eyes were as beautiful as yours."

"Your wife?" She spoke the words in a steady whisper.

The question made him want to talk, and he told her briefly about Nyoman Puri.

"I'm sorry, I've made you sad."

They were interrupted by the voice of the flight attendant advising passengers to fasten their seat belts because they were running into turbulence. I Wayan stretched out and closed his eyes. He heard the woman beside him whispering prayers.

When the turbulence had passed, she took up the conversation where they had left off.

"I don't only want to be a dancer like Nyoman Puri. I want to be a leader in the women's movement." She spoke the words with conviction, smiling at the same time.

"Like the Acehnese heroine Cut Nyak Dien? Or Kartini in Java? Mother Teresa? Or Britain's iron woman, Margaret Thatcher?"

"No, not like them. I want to be myself as a leader. There are more and more regulations these days that put women into cages. No matter that this is supposed to be an age of reform."

"Do we really have discriminatory regulations against women?" I Wayan's voice took on a teasing edge.

"Are you testing me?" Her lips were smiling, but there was a challenge in her eyes.

"Great! You've got a dream. Actions start with dreams."

"Not the other way around?"

"The other way is to go to sleep and dream, like lots of the big shots in this country of yours." They looked at each other. The plane shook as it ran into a thick bank of cloud. The flight attendant again asked the passengers to fasten their seat belts.

"Thanks for the chat." I Wayan spoke over the announcement.

"I've enjoyed it, too." She extended her hand. "I'm *Cut* Anie."

"It's really your eyes that do a lot of the talking."

"That's what my husband says, too. He tells me to keep looking straight ahead when I go anywhere, not to look at the people around me." She laughed good-naturedly.

"So is that what you do?"

"How can I?"

They kept on talking as they left the plane and headed for the baggage claim area. It turned out they were booked on the same plane back to the capital.

"Watch what you do with those eyes!" I Wayan whispered.

And the eyes answered him, like the surface of a lake swept by a passing breeze.

One week later, at four in the afternoon, I Wayan was back in the check-in line at the airport. When it came to his turn to get a boarding pass, he also requested a seat for *Cut* Anie.

In the boarding area, he kept sitting down then standing up again and walking around, seeking out those rolling eyes. He took note of every woman whose head and neck were covered in a scarf. In fact there were only two or three women there wearing scarves. All the rest wore the Islamic headdress or left their heads uncovered. The boarding call came. He stood up, his eyes still roving about in search of the eyes that flashed with fire.

Finally there she was. But the eyes he'd been searching for were hidden behind impenetrable dark glasses.

"What's up with your eyes? Are they sore?"

"No," she whispered. On the way out to the plane she told him that her husband had asked her to wear dark glasses to stop people looking at her eyes. Because her eyes belonged to him alone.

Once she was seated on the plane, she took the glasses off. They sat for a long time without speaking, without even stealing a look at each other. All the while their chests heaved.

"Are you feeling sad?" she asked suddenly.

"No."

"Why don't you look at my eyes?"

"Didn't you say they belonged to your husband?"

"He owns the dark glasses, not my eyes."

She held back a laugh. The dance instructor who wanted to be a leader in the women's movement was prodding the man old enough to be her father into taking a subtle look into the fullness of her eyes.

Home

I missed home. I wanted to go home. I was going home…
Suddenly I sprang from my sleep and sat cross-legged on the
mattress, the sheet still covering my lower body from waist
to toes. But there, still very clear before my eyes, was the face of
the dancer, the *joged* dancer, who tapped me on the shoulder with
her fan. At first she had approached another man in the audience,
in the far corner of the performance space, but then, suddenly,
twirling and fluttering her arms like the wings of a bee, she came
towards me.

The crowd roared its approval: "Yes, him! Him!"

She then tapped me with her fan and handed me her *selendang*,
the dance sash draped from the tips of her fingers. Moving
sensuously, she signaled for me to follow her to the central dance
space. Not moving from my side, her arms moving like those of a
bird in flight, she waited for to follow.

"Dance! Dance with her!"

The cries of the audience were a thunderous wave that left me
bewitched as I was pulled into a whirlpool of mystery. The people
seated beside me pushed me towards the dance arena and I danced
as if in a trance, not conscious of my body as it moved in dance.
Though the cries of the audience were louder than the music of the
bamboo gamelan, I was able to follow the rhythmic tapping on
the *kempul*, suspended gongs whose reverberating sound steered
my hips and turned my behind. When I managed to glance at
the cheering crowd, I was stunned, for most of them were people

I knew who had been killed in the great slaughter of 1965. Then looking my more closely at the face of the *joged* dancer, whose cheeks were now flirtatiously close to mine, I saw that she was a classmate who once used to flirt with me in junior and senior high school.

"Sartini? Is that you?" I mumbled as if to myself.

Sartini batted her lashes, her eyes darting to the left and right. Her lips curled into a smile. She moved her arms and the *selendang* hanging from them rose and fell, just like a butterfly's wings. She left my side, dancing into the distance until finally she was swallowed by darkness.

I tried to scream, to call out her name, but no sound issued from my throat.

Startled speechless and sweating, I immediately awoke, gasping for breath.

My wife, Kasih, stirred beneath the blanket where she lay coiled in sleep. "What's wrong?"

I couldn't immediately answer. My ears still rang with the sound of bamboo gamelan, guiding my body and that of Sartini as we, trancelike, danced the *joged*. Strangely, the dance floor itself was moving, like waves on the ocean. I glimpsed a familiar shore where pandanus flowers grew. I knew that stretch of shoreline, a beach known as Kubu Gembong; I sometimes used to camp there for a night or two, when I was a teenager. When on vacation between school terms it was a favorite destination for members of the Young Students Association in my village. The sea was gentle and the waves were soft; and at night, beneath the light of a full moon, we would sing and dance to the music of a gamelan whose instruments were the voices of the young revelers. Some of the boys would practice *silat*, the dance-like martial art, sparring with one another. Laughter was infectious as we pushed and pulled on those friends who were embarrassed to dance.

"I want to go home." My voice cracked as I spoke.

"Home? But we are home. This is our home." Kasih sounded exasperated.

"I want to go *home*."

"What, to Bogor?"

"No, home," I said yet again.

"Fifty years and you still don't feel like your home is here, like this is your own home,"

Only half awake, I said nothing to this. The face of the *joged* dancer was still there, in front of my eyes. Her bright eyes flashed, darting back and forth with the whistling music of a bamboo flute. The faces of my dead friends were also there. I breathed slowly, taking in deep breaths.

"I want to go home to Banjar Tegal."

Kasih sat up and flattened her hair against the back of her head. "What is it? Did you have a dream?"

I told her of the dream that still drugged my consciousness.

Finally, she said to me: "All right then, go home. But when? Today?"

"I don't know. I have to think about it."

"How many years has it been and you still can't leave that world behind. How long will this go on? If you're not dreaming of being in prison, you dream of being hunted by the security forces. You're forever dreaming of your friends who died and the intelligence officers who arrested you. You're still a prisoner, a victim of your past. Be careful, you're likely to bring on an asthma attack."

I didn't reply. I was silent because what Kasih had said was true.

"Maybe it was because you played that *joged* gamelan music last night and it went into your dream?"

"Could be," I answered slowly.

Kasih said soothingly: "The spirits of your friends still think of you. They want you to pray for them." Pulling the blanket over herself, she burrowed back into the bed.

I chose a window seat on the plane. I always chose a window seat when I went home to Bali. Not so, when I returned to Java; I didn't want to see the Balinese shoreline, with its foam-tipped breakers, recede into the distance. As soon as it was announced that the plane would be landing soon, my eyes sought the approaching land mass. First scanning the great blue expanse, my eyes then found the shore, its foam-tipped edge like a dance scarf of snow wrapped around the island's waistline. This sight lifted me, taking my mind to the nether distance, making me feel I never wanted to leave Bali again.

I planned to soak in the sea, in the morning just when the new sun begins to tiptoe across the rooftops. I would call on Ketut Mirta, the only friend of mine from those days still living. When we were in high school, we often took turns staying overnight at each other's house. I wanted to see a *joged* performance as well and hoped that someone would be holding a ceremony for which they'd hire a *joged* troupe. There were so many things I wanted to do, I hoped to spend at least a month in Bali. I hoped to find Dayu Nur, the Brahman girl I'd had my eye on in high school but never succeeded in getting to be my girlfriend because she was already hooked up with a Brahman boy. She later married that young man, but in 1966 he was murdered by security forces. The last time I had seen Dayu Nur was when I returned home in the 1980s. We had poured out our hearts to each other then.

My plan was to stay at the home of my nephew, the son of my older brother, whose home was only about half a kilometer from the beach.

My older sister, the second child in the family, lived with her husband in a house next to that of our brother. In fact, to get to my nephew's house, you had to pass through my sister's house.

As I approached the house that day of my return, I craned my neck to see who might be there. From a distance, I could see my sister's husband standing outside the house. He was dressed in a dirty T-shirt and long shorts that went to his calves.

I approached him. "Hi, *Bli*, what are you up to?"

"Post office…"

"What, you're waiting for a letter from one of the boys?"

"Post office…" he repeated.

My sister then appeared. Her face was dull and her eyes glistened with tears.

"Did you just arrive?" she said right away. "Will you be staying here?"

"Nah, next door, I think. But what's with *Bli*? He just keeps saying says 'post office'."

"This is what I'm going through."

"What do you mean?"

"That's what he does almost every day. He comes out here and stands, saying that he's going to the post office. He used to work there, you know, but was let go without notice. He says he's going to demand his pension and always keeps asking, over and over, why he was fired when he wasn't involved in anything at all."

"So then what happens?"

"Nothing. He just keeps standing there until I come out and promise that I'll take him to the post office. Only then will he come inside." My sister's voice caught in her throat.

I could barely keep my own voice under control as I invited my brother-in-law to go inside: "Come on in, *Bli*, I'll take you to the post office later."

He turned slowly, and walked ever so slowly towards the house, as if a heavy metal chain were wrapped around his ankles.

I slept soundly that night, as if in my mother's lap, but very early the next morning I was awakened by the loud sound of the first call to prayer coming from over a loudspeaker. Was I in Bali, I wondered, only half conscious, but then, a few hours later, I heard coming from the distance, the soft sound of people praying the *Trisandya*, inviting the Hindu flock to prayer when the sun came up.

"That's right," I thought, "here they live beside each other in their differences."

That first morning I went down to the beach to soak in the sea. When I returned home, I stopped at my sister's house where we talked about her two children, who were now college graduates with jobs.

"The kids think of us, I'm sure," my sister told me; "It's just that the jobs they found are way off in Kalimantan and Lombok. When I Kadek comes home he rents a car and takes his father for a ride, wherever he wants to go. I Wayan doesn't make so much, so he can only show his father affection through the little gifts he brings for him."

"But that's something," I commented.

"That's true, I suppose. After the incident, you know, we had to work hard, going from one harvest place to the next selling the porridge, to make sure that the boys could get a college degree— even if they wouldn't get a job with the government; it would have been useless to even try. Just look at what happened to their father. That pension of his. I'm tired of telling him to stop trying."

"Didn't do anything and they fired me," said my brother-in-law, his voice broken, his tongue stiff. "Where's my pension?"

"When they interrogated him, he just shut up, said nothing. Maybe he was riled for being accused of all sorts of things, so he just said nothing at all. Because of that, they said he was part of what they called *Gerakan Tutup Mulut*, the 'Sealed Lips Movement'.

"It made me nervous every time they came to the house to talk to him. But I was so relieved they didn't take him away."

Every morning, after the sun came up, I'd go to the beach for therapy. That's what I called it, basking in the therapeutic rays of the sun and bathing in the warm sea water. The air was clean, the beach far from the dust and pollution of the road. In the evening, I'd often find myself staring at Mount Gilimanuk, which faced Mount Banyuwangi across the strait. The two peaks were tied together by a yellowish-red streak, like a dance scarf thrown across the two mountains' shoulders. Mesmerized by the changing light, I'd fall into twilight's embrace. I'd feel nature's warmth infuse my body and my soul, giving me calmness, stimulating a sense of hope. This was my home; the sea and the sun were my parents, my lover, my forbearers to whom I addressed my complaints and from whom I sought advice on how to go ahead. This was a feeling I never found at Ancol Beach in Jakarta or at Carita on Java's northwestern shore. This was something my wife, the descendent of gentry from Solo, a city far from the sea in Java's interior, never understood at all.

"The beach is so much dirtier than it used to be," I complained one morning as we nibbled on a mid-morning snack.

"People throw trash in the sea and the sea throws it back onto the beach," said one of my young relatives.

"Then let's clean it up," I briskly suggested.

"You clean it today, and tomorrow it's full of trash again," my nephew answered.

"Well, if we don't do it, who will?"

"Yeah, who?" he said.

"If I lived here, I'd spend part of my mornings cleaning the beach with whoever else was around and wanted to help. I'd ask you kids and other people who were down at the beach."

"How much would you pay?"

I laughed in reply and then invited them to come swimming with me at the beach.

I got my hope of seeing a *joged* performance: one of the villagers whose son was getting married hired a *joged* troupe to perform at the wedding reception.

"Are you going to dance with the *joged*?" asked one of my grand-nieces who was going to watch the performance.

"Can you do that, Uncle? Are you good at it?" asked another as she dressed.

"Of course, I can. I used to be a *baris* dancer at the village temple. I could dance the *jauk*, and do *pencak silat*, too. "

We were late in arriving at the communal hall where the *joged* performance was being held, and found that it had already begun. The person next to me quickly informed me, however, that the top dancer had yet to appear. That was usually the case: the prima donna never took the stage before the audience had reached its capacity. If four or five dancers were performing, she would dance third or fourth, in the middle of the show.

As soon as the second dancer had finished, someone called out "Sari Kuning! Sari Kuning", apparently the name of that night's top dancer. The cry was picked up by others until all were yelling Sari Kuning's name. Their shouts were answered by the explosive sound of strikers on bamboo, which overpowered the human cries, causing them to recede and drown. All eyes of the audience were on the curtain from behind which Sari Kuning would emerge.

As soon as her face appeared through the gap between the curtains, her fingers moving the cloth aside to the beat of the gamelan, people called and whistled. Sari Kuning didn't dance the *joged* in the normal style; she writhed in the manner of Inul Daratista, the *dangdut* singer who was as famous for her sensuality as for her vocal skills. Her movements were those of a belly dancer. Her brilliant smile and flashing eyes excited passion. Men waved their hands in the air, signaling that they wanted to be chosen to dance with her.

Sari Kuning finally made her choice, and the young man who accepted her dance scarf followed her to the central dance arena. From the very start, his body mimicked Sari Kuning's erotic movements. They were a mare and a stallion just released from their pens, she in heat and he in pursuit. Urged on by the cries and clapping of the audience, they mimed the movements of a couple in the throes of passion. Their bodies brushed against each other, their hands entwined; they attacked and fell back, attacked but always giving the other one the chance to pursue.

The dancer who followed Sari Kuning was even more lascivious, and you could hardly call her performance a *joged* dance. As if taking the cue from Sari Kuning, her performance was a demonstration of how to flirt, how to kiss, and how to make love.

By the time I arrived home that evening, I was tired and felt out of breath. I immediately lay down. "Where am I?" I asked myself. "Am I in Bali?" All of a sudden, I felt a twinge of memory. "Is this still the village I once called home?"

The next day my nephew took me to the home of Ketut Mirta, the only friend of mine who had survived the incident. I was told he was at his paddy field, keeping the birds from devouring his crop. His daughter-in-law showed me the way to his field. Walking atop the dikes that divided the fields took me back to my childhood— that and the sound of running water in the trench, the smell of the soil, the expanse of ripened paddy, and the bamboo poles to which pieces of cloth were tied as scarecrows for the birds. I heard the shout of a woman scaring off a bird trying to land in her field. The tinkling sound of makeshift bells made from metal cans made me realize that I was in the land of my youth, the womb that had given birth to me.

I called out to Ketut Mirta and he came to where I was standing, in the shade of a rosewood tree at the edge of the paddy field.

I shook his hand and said enthusiastically: "Hello! Still remember me?"

Ketut Mirta shook his head, unsure.

"I used to stay overnight at your house and you would stay at mine."

"Just a second…"

"We used to play rummy together."

"Not Widya?"

"Widya was murdered."

"I Toya?"

"He's dead too."

"I Kaler?"

"He hung himself."

"Who else was there?" As if his sight had dimmed, he felt my body with his hands, then stared hard at me, but still didn't seem to find the answer.

"Don't you remember pushing me to go after Dayu Nur?"

With that comment, Ketut Mirta suddenly burst into laughter. "Oh my God, it's you? Of course, I didn't recognize you. How could I? Look at how big you've gotten. You used to be skinnier than a chicken bone."

He slapped my body with the palms of his hands. He stroked my head and then raised my hands as if to look for something. Suddenly, he began to cry. With a wrinkled hand, black from the sun and with bulging veins, he brushed the tears from his eyes. He then embraced me.

"I once heard that you survived, but why didn't you ever come home?"

"I came back before, but I just never got the chance to look for you."

In the shelter of the rosewood tree, we let ourselves be taken back to the past. Ketut told me of the horror he had felt at the time of the incident, when anyone thought to be a leftist was slaughtered. He had only survived, he told me, because he had an uncle influential enough to guarantee that Ketut was not a communist.

At one point, I told him: "Every day since I've been here, I go down to the beach, to the place where we used to camp, to soak in the waves."

He seemed surprised by my comment and the enjoyment I found there on that beach.

He paused, as if wanted to say something. Finally, his voice trembling, he said, "You don't know, do you?"

"Know what?"

He lowered his voice. "That's where our friends were killed and buried, including Sartini, who they raped first. A few months ago, there was an awful storm and churned up the shoreline so badly that it exposed a mess of bones."

"And then...?" I could only whisper, my voice lost in my throat.

He rose from where he was sitting, then stood and looked at me. His eyes were sharp; his lips trembled.

"The next time you come home, come visit me. Maybe I'll still be alive." He then turned and walked away. Not long afterwards I heard his clear voice cutting through the sky, chasing away the birds that were landing on the paddy stalks.

I didn't go to the beach after that. My blood pressure rose; I became short of breath. The longing that I had felt before my visit had vanished. After seven days, I sent a text message to my wife.

"I want to come home."

"You're in Bali," she texted back. "What other home do you have?"

"Your lap."

"Such a flirt and a jerk!"

"I'm serious."

"Where are you now?"

"Boarding the plane at Ngurah Rai."

Publishing Data for the Stories and their Translations

"The Paper Round" was first published, in Indonesian, under the title "Loper", in *Harian Rakyat* (March 8, 1964); English translation by Keith Foulcher.

"Pan Blayag" was first published, in Indonesian, under the same title, in *Sinar Harapan*, (March 25, 1979); English translation by Leslie Dwyer.

"Storm Clouds over the Island of Paradise" was first published, in Indonesian, under the title "Mega Hitam Pulau Kayangan", in *Luh Galuh* (Jakarta: Goethe Instituut, 1987) and later republished in *Keringat Mutiara* (Jakarta: Kalyanamitra, 1991). The English translation, by Vern Cork, first appeared in *Another Kind of Paradise: Short Stories from the New Asia Pacific* (Boston: Cheng & Tsui Co., 2010).

"The Bag" was first published, in Indonesian, under the title "*Tas*" in *Luh Galuh: Kumpulan Cerita Pendek* (Jakarta: Goethe Instituut, 1986); English translation by Keith Foulcher.

"Luh Galuh" was first published, in Indonesian, under the same title, in *Femina*, 1987, then later republished in *Luh Galuh: Kumpulan Cerita Pendek* (Jakarta: Goethe Institut, 1987) and in *Keringat Mutiara* (Jakarta: Kalyanamitra, 1991). The English translation, by Mary Zurbuchen, first appeared in *Menagerie 4* (Jakarta: Lontar, 2000).

"Bridge of Light" was first published, in Indonesian, under the title "Jembatan Cahaya" in *Rindu Terluka* (Jakarta: Metafor, 2004).

The English translation, by Keith Foulcher, first appeared in *Wounded Longing* (Bandung: Ultimus, 2010).

"Wounded Longing" was first published, in Indonesian, under the title "Rindu Terluka", in *Rindu Terluka* (Jakarta: Metafor, 2004). The English translation, by Keith Foulcher, first appeared in *Wounded Longing* (Bandung: Ultimus, 2010).

"He Wept in Front of the TV" was first published, in Indonesian, under the title "Ia Menangis di Depan Televisi", in *Bukan Kematian* (Yogyakarta: Ombak, 2006); English translation by Keith Foulcher.

"Letter of Invitation" was first published, in Indonesian, under the title "Surat Undangan", in *Kompas* (July 24, 2005), then later republished in *Bukan Kematian* (Yogyakarta: Ombak, 2006); English translation by Keith Foulcher.

"Nita" was first published, in Indonesian, under the same title, in *Titian: Antologi Cerita Pendek Kerakyatan* (Depok: Koekoesan, 2008); English translation by Keith Foulcher.

"Eyes" was first published, in Indonesian, under the title "Mata", in the journal *Perempuan* (No.70, July 2011); English translation by Keith Foulcher.

"Home" was first published, in Indonesian, under the title "Pulang", in *Takkan Melupakanmu* (Jakarta: Jaker-LKK, 2012); English translation by John H. McGlynn.

The Author

Putu Oka Sukanta was born in Singaraja, northern Bali, in 1939, and has been active as a writer since the age of sixteen. From 1966 until 1976, he was a political prisoner following the military coup d'état that brought General Suharto to power. He has since been invited overseas for theater performances, poetry readings, and  literary conferences in Sri Lanka, Bangladesh, Australia, Malaysia, Germany, and France. His works include children's books, three collections of poetry, and two volumes of short stories. He works as an acupuncturist and has also written on alternative medicine.

The Translators & Other Contributors

Vern Cork, an Australian teacher and librarian, has been involved with Bali in a variety of roles since his first visit in 1972: public library development advisor, community development worker, co-founder of two foundations for Balinese with disabilities, and translator of Indonesian literature about Bali. His literary translations include *Bali Behind the Seen* (recent fiction from Bali by Balinese writers; *The Sweat of Pearls*, stories about women of Bali by Putu Oka Sukanta; *Ordeal by Fire*, a collection of stories by Aryantha Soethama; and *Songs of the Heart*, poems by Balinese with disabilities.

Leslie Dwyer is Director of the Center for the Study of Gender and Conflict at the School for Conflict Analysis and Resolution at George Mason University in Arlington, Virginia, U.S. She is a cultural anthropologist with a PhD from Princeton University who has been working in Indonesia since 1993. Her research focuses on issues of violence, gender, post-conflict social life, transitional justice, and the politics of memory and identity.

Keith Foulcher is an Honorary Associate of the Department of Indonesian Studies at the University of Sydney. Before his retirement in 2006 he taught Indonesian language and literature at the University of Sydney, and previously held positions at Monash University and Flinders University. His major research interests and publications are in the field of modern Indonesian literature and cultural history, especially of the late colonial and early independence periods.

John MacDougall is a cultural anthropologist and student of books on human rights, Indonesian labor movements, gang militancy, Indonesian Buddhism, Balinese Hinduism and minority religions in Indonesia. He first started coming to Indonesia in 1988 and has followed and participated in monitoring political activism and state violence against minorities in China, Indonesia and East Timor. He continues to write on religious and political leadership among Indonesian minorities and religious rituals in areas of high infant mortality.

John H. McGlynn is a long-term resident of Indonesia, having lived in Jakarta almost continually since 1976. He is the translator of several dozen publications under his own name, and through the Lontar Foundation, which he established with four Indonesian authors in 1987, has brought into print more than one hundred books on Indonesian literature and culture.

Degung Santikarma is an anthropologist and human rights activist. He and Leslie Dwyer have together conducted ten years of research on the 1965-66 violence and its cultural and political aftermath in Bali.

Mary Zurbuchen is a Southeast Asia specialist and independent researcher who currently serves as Director for Asia and Russia of the Ford Foundation International Fellowships Program (IFP). From 1992-2000 she was the Southeast Asia Regional Representative and Representative for Indonesia in the Ford Foundation's Jakarta office. She has taught Southeast Asian Studies at the University of California, and her published work includes *The Language of Balinese Shadow Theater* and *Beginning to Remember: The Past in the Indonesian Present*, an edited volume of studies on historical memory in Indonesia.